N.D. 48 Sojourner
A Novel of the New Dispensation

Rachel Winters

Copyright © 2016 Rachel Winters

This book, or parts thereof, may not be reproduced in any form without permission. For information address parasigil66@gmail.com.

Published by: Parasigil Press, The Villages, Florida

ISBN: 0-9983437-3-0 / 978-0-9983437-3-0

Library of Congress Catalog Card Number: 2016918987

First Paperback Edition

Printed in the U.S.A.

Also available as an e-book from Amazon.com.

DEDICATION

For all those wonderful people who read my first book and urged me to write a second: Michael, of course, Douglas, C.J., Barry, Karl, Nancy, Gary L., De. Here it is. I hope you love it.

ACKNOWLEDGMENTS

Beaucoup thanks are due Nancy Corder, friend and, fortuitously, editor extraordinaire. Your input made this a better book.

At the beginning of the New Dispensation, the Conclave of Elders had taken responsibility for bringing order amidst the chaos of a devastating worldwide plague. In N.D. 48, the 48th year of the New Dispensation, following upon the events chronicled previously in N.D. 47, challenges emerge to their benevolent autocracy including the rise of a militant religious cult and a spot of deep science gone awry.

1

The lake is deep
The water cold
The ancient stones
Indifferent

Chandler Besdine's eyes filled with tears as he stroked his thumb over the words incised in the crude clay urn holding his grandfather's ashes. The poem had been written by his ancestor and cut into the surface by Chandler himself.

His grandfather was a great man, wise and ruthless. He taught his grandson about their bloodline, the bloodline of rulers. He taught him to use the fighting ball. And he taught Chandler how the Conclave betrayed himself and the world. He stressed to his grandson the necessity for vengeance. Chandler adored and respected him. When he died, Chandler inherited his ashes and his mission. And the unyielding guilt that came from letting his beloved ancestor die alone.

After several years of frustration, Chandler was finally in a position to take crucial steps that would significantly advance their mission. For that, he needed Ana Bede, or her mentor, Dr. Desmond Elvistine. Chandler was not sure he believed Ana's story about Elvistine and the portal. It didn't matter. Ana would be as useful as Elvistine, maybe more. And he had arranged with his superiors in the Conclave of Elders to be given responsibility for a project in the now-dead city where his grandfather had lived and worked. A project that would fit perfectly in his plan for their destruction.

To take both important actions, he needed help and he knew just the citizen to enlist.

Arlo Gauss was squatting in his old friends Colt and Ana's flat in the city while they were in Deep Cove dealing with her grief at the loss of her mentor. Sometime previously, Arlo had returned to the city from exile to take care of Ana, having heard on good authority that she was in danger from radical anti-ephemerists. Before he could do anything, however, Ana, her husband, Colt, and their old friends and flatmates Teegan and Jordi Petrie had ended up in Deep Cove, a small village on the coast some distance from the city. Arlo had heard only rumors about the dramatic events at Deep Cove. Ana, at least, seemed safe. Comm frequencies were heavily monitored by the authorities and, outside major population centers, unreliable. At any rate, he had been unable to reach Deep Cove.

While he enjoyed one of Colt's bottles of wine, he contemplated his options. Having Chandler Besdine open the door and saunter into his temporary flat was distinctly unpleasant.

"Citizen Gauss," Chandler slouched into an armchair and tossed his head. The fighting ball that was woven into the end of his long braid settled into place on his chest.

Arlo said nothing. Chandler was always bad news.

"Citizen Gauss," Chandler repeated. "Let's discuss how you are going to get out of the deep, deep trouble you are in."

"Deep, deep," Arlo repeated, trying to sound wry and insoucient; regretting, not for the first time, that he was not the type to carry a weapon. The assertion he made so often in his youth—that a brain was better than a weapon—seemed pretty silly at the moment.

"You know," Chandler continued conversationally, crossing his legs, "the bounty on you has never been lifted. If you were identified and turned over to the authorities, you would be sent to the stasis chamber immediately, no questions asked.

"You are, or were at one time, a sworn enemy of the Conclave. Your cabal, under the direction of Professor Tillman, were dedicated to fighting the stranglehold—your word—that the Conclave have on world society. Your group blew things up. Citizens died. Innocent citizens. And none of their deaths made any difference in the conclave's relentless grip, as you always termed it, on the world. No citizens, anywhere, rose up to challenge the iron fists of the elders."

"We were being manipulated, lied to." Arlo said, enraged, as he usually was when he was forced to remember that he and his group of student revolutionists were being used as assassins.

Chandler went into the kitchen and returned with a wine glass, helping himself from the bottle on the coffee table.

"Get a grip Arlo," Chandler said, after a while. "You were used and you were fingered. But I'm not going to turn you in. I need your cooperation. If you help me, I can guarantee you will be free in the future to do whatever you like without fear of reprisals from anyone."

"You are in the Conclave, aren't you?" Arlo was still angry.

"My family is in the consistory." The consistory was composed of old families who carried out the directives of the Conclave of Elders and managed the details associated with running the world.

"Members of the Conclave come from the consistory."

Chandler laughed. "I'm hardly old enough to be an elder."

Arlo didn't think that was necessarily true. Rumor said the C.E. were big on merit admissions.

"What do you want me to do?"

"Before I tell you, I want to make it clear that I am completely and unreservedly loyal to the Conclave. Just for your information, now and in the future."

Arlo doubted this statement, but made no comment, just nodded slightly.

"It's some religionists, isn't it?" Arlo was suddenly enlightened. "They have finally got critical mass to move against you."

Chandler laughed, highly amused. "Maybe. These are dangerous times."

"Or is it the protestors? I heard weapons were

being moved into their camp." Arlo was referring to a group of citizens who had set up a kind of shantytown on a large section of wasteland within the city and near the university and its Institute of Temporal Epistemology formerly directed by Dr. Elvistine. Their agenda seemed to be anti-ephemerist, the term they used for the theoretical, or deep, science studied by the staff of the institute. The protestors seemed to blame ephemerists for the plague that had wiped out a large portion of the population of the planet and everything bad that had come after it.

"Piet Lem no doubt told you about the weapons." Chandler didn't bother to confirm with Arlo the source of his information.

"He isn't happy about it," Arlo said.

"No, his organization, and those like it, are happiest when they are the only ones in the area with weapons."

Arlo said, "As far as I know, Piet and his people couldn't find out who was providing the arms to the protestors and what they aimed to accomplish. The protestors seem to be just a group of none-to-bright anti-ephemerists."

Chandler smirked. "Possibly they see themselves as the grassroots warriors who will restore the world to a pre-plague paradise."

"Like we were trying to do," Arlo said slowly.

"Exactly."

"And they are also being used, as we were?"

"What do you think?"

Arlo shrugged.

"What do you want me to do?"

"I want you to go to Dr. Ana Bede and then

contact me. I promise you nothing bad will happen to her."

"Why is everyone after Ana? She's just a scientist."

Chandler frowned. "As to other citizens who are searching for Ana, I have no information." He didn't look too happy with this idea. "For myself, I want her to close the portal that she and Elvistine opened within the institute."

"Why?"

"I think it's dangerous."

"You still believe it is a black hole," Arlo tried not to sneer.

Chandler refused to be drawn. "Just find Ana, and you will be okay."

Arlo looked surprised. "You can find her yourself. She and Colt are in Deep Cove. He is anxious to return to the city but she's all broken up about Elvistine's death."

"I know. I was there when she announced that he had disappeared through a portal he opened up in his hospital room."

"I hadn't heard that," Arlo was surprised.

"She also said it was the beginning of Armageddon."

Arlo was shocked. He had to think where he had heard the term. Perhaps in a class about old belief systems. Before he could comment on this outrageous statement, Chandler said, "Nothing that Ana claimed is for public dissemination or important, for that matter. I want you to go to Deep Cove and make sure she stays there until I can send for her."

"You think she and Elvistine developed a protocol for closing the portal?"

"I hope so. Elvistine was not able to do it before

he left us, however he left us. I doubt very much that he opened a portal in his hospital room."

"Why not?"

"Because manipulating a portal would require vast quantities of fusion power, certainly not available in a rural hospital room."

"What do you think happened to him? Why would Ana lie?"

"I plan to ask her."

With that he sauntered out of the flat, leaving Arlo confounded.

He sank onto the sofa, his head in his hands. He needed to contact Colt and Ana immediately, to warn them. If necessary, he would have to go to Deep Cove. For that, he would need the help of his friend, Piet Lem and Grupo Uno.

2

Piet Lem and his son Beau were back in the Subs, as the vast network of tunnels and caverns under the bedrock of the city was called. Piet was relieved. Maybe now things would get back to normal in their life, his and Beau's. There were some troubling reports from his lieutenants in Grupo Uno about unusual goings on in the Subs, but Piet had lived in the Subs most of his life and something was always going on. Most recently arms were being funneled through the Subs to the protestors who had established a camp in the city.

He wondered if Irene Thorne had been involved with arming the protestors. As far as he had known, his and Irene's paths had never crossed before the debacle in Deep Cove. Then she had said, shortly before she had died, that Rowan was reporting to her on their movements. The unanswered question was why she was spying on his activities. He had no intention of interfering with the flow of arms unless they presented a direct threat to him or his people in

Grupo Uno.

As usual Arlo Gauss seemed to be the catalyst for bad things happening to Piet Lem. Before Arlo had returned from exile to warn Colt's wife Ana about some still unspecified threat, Irene Thorne was unknown to either of them. Arlo was a very old friend and fellow religionist, but he was always a focal point of trouble.

Piet had met Ana's husband Colt, then known as Colt Desormeaux, through Arlo when they were at university together. Piet had closely followed Colt's career as a champion cage fighter and kept in touch when Colt retired to the city, entered into a sanctioned relationship with Ana Bede, assumed her surname, and devoted himself to gambling. Colt was a good guy, if a little dim, and Piet had been willing to help when Arlo said Colt's wife Ana was in some kind of trouble. Arlo said someone, and no one had yet discovered who or why, wanted to harm her. Piet had hidden her in the Subs and his son Beau had volunteered to accompany her to the countryside when Dr. Elvistine was attacked by bandits and injured on a trip to the Citadel where the Conclave of Elders resided. Piet had been proud of Beau for volunteering since his experiences in the dangerous countryside were limited. He had been even more impressed at his son's stoicism and self-control when Irene Thorne and her thug had threatened them at gunpoint at the villa in Deep Cove.

Irene had known where they were because Beau's girlfriend Rowan had been snitching on them to Irene. Piet leaned back in his chair and watched Beau and Rowan prepare dinner. Beau had matured over the previous few weeks. He had experienced his first extended trip out of the city to the coastal village of Deep Cove and witnessed the violent death of two people. He was handling himself well, now, interacting with Rowan, who had reportedly betrayed them to an enemy.

Piet had been in favor of getting their business associate Yonatan Belasco to administer some of the potent psychoactive truth drugs he used as a professional re-educator but, interestingly, Beau had proposed a more subtle approach. They would lull her into a sense of security with food and wine, then attempt to coax her into discussing her involvement with the older woman. Irene had been smitten with another young girl, Colt's protégé, Linnet, and Beau thought she might have been attracted to Rowan as well. He thought they might get Rowan talking about her acquaintance with Irene. They would like to know how Rowan and Irene met, for example. Rowan had been found as an infant toddling naked in the Subs, adopted by a member of Grupo Uno, and as far as anyone in the group knew, had never been upside in the city. Nor had anyone reported seeing Irene in the Subs.

Beau had outdone himself, ordering platters of rice pilaf with high-quality, succulent soy scallops and marinated vegetables from one of the Subs' best food kiosks. Piet had contributed a bottle of excellent sparkling wine that he thought would appeal to the girl's, presumably naïve, palate. It had worked, too. The young girl was guzzling the wine with delight and had begun eating the marinated vegetables with her fingers.

Piet contented himself with eating the delicious food, drinking tea, and watching his son manipulate the conversation. Beau was flirting with Rowan, leaning in, complimenting her. When he thought the time was right, he said, "I didn't know you had ever been upside."

"I haven't," she had replied. "I've lived downside all my life, at least as far as I remember."

"That's funny," Beau had said, innocently, "because I met someone the other day who said she knows you and I don't think she has ever been in the Subs." He paused. "Irene Thorne," he said, taking a sip of wine.

"Irene's dead," the girl said flatly, no longer giggling.

Piet and Beau exchanged glances. The number of people who should know that was severely limited.

Piet started to say something, but Beau merely said, off-handedly, "Are you sure? We were just with her recently."

"I'm sure." The girl looked wary.

"Wow, really? Who told you that? I hadn't heard it."

"I just heard it, that's all."

"From someone in the Subs?" Piet couldn't help saying.

Her hand was shaking as she set the wineglass on the table.

"I better go." She started to stand up but Beau put a hand on her shoulder and kept her in her seat.

"Maybe it was just a rumor," she hung her head, not looking at them.

Piet put a finger under her chin, lifting her face to his. "Look at me, Rowan. Who have you been keeping company with that you hear rumors about citizens like Irene Thorne? Was it from your uncle?"

Her adoptive uncle was one of Piet's trusted lieutenants.

The girl looked shocked then shook her head, looking away from them.

"Then who?"

She shook her head again.

"You want to tell us why you were giving Irene information about Grupo Uno?"

She continued to look down, shaking her head.

"Did your uncle put you up to it?"

"No, no. I told you no."

Piet stood up. "You know what you did was very dangerous, betraying your family."

She started to cry.

"Are you going to hurt me?"

Piet didn't answer. Beau stood by, stoically holding her in her chair.

Piet turned away, and Beau began to speak to her, softly. He assured her that she would not be hurt, not be punished, if she answered their questions. Still she refused to speak. Piet had known her all her life and as head of Grupo Uno, he had been the most powerful person in her world, and yet she did not trust him.

Piet became increasingly frustrated. Finally, he had said to Beau, "Enough of this. Get Yonatan Belasco. Go. Now." Beau had merely nodded and, a true child of the Subs, vanished into the darkness.

3

Yonatan Belasco was trying to enjoy a gathering at the home of a prominent city family, the kind of people, he reminded himself, he was most comfortable with, the kind he had been reared among. He should feel relaxed, at home. Instead he felt out of sorts. He rarely indulged himself in such socializing because in his role as a sanctioned re-educator he found it useful to be aloof, to keep his distance. Still the hostess was one of his oldest friends and all the guests were completely vetted and deemed acceptable by the city's elite. Many of the guests were known to be intimates of the Conclave of Elders. There was a scattering of strangers, among them a native of the area spoken of as the land of volcanoes, notable for his characteristic, but sanctioned, ground-sweeping tunic.

Earlier in the evening Yonatan had briefly considered inviting one of Sparrow's high-end courtesans to be his companion at the party. He had reluctantly decided against it. His commitment to celibacy wavered whenever he visited Sparrow's sanctioned sex club, the House of Blue Leaves. Sex wasn't the issue anyway. He was feeling lonely, even among so many old friends. As a healer who specialized in the mind, he knew this feeling was a function of his age and his decision to pursue the occasionally dangerous career of a re-educator. As a young practitioner, he had concluded that entering into a sanctioned relationship would be unfair because it could be potentially dangerous for the other party. Now, as an experienced practitioner, he wondered if he just lacked guts. He had thought, maybe, here, among his friends, he might find someone; but none of the citizens at the party were as sympathetic, as richly welcoming and intriguing as his friend's best employees.

The party was in a beautifully restored penthouse encircled by windows that looked down upon the lights of the city. The pall that usually hung over the landscape had providentially lifted to allow the guests to enjoy the sight of the moon glowing within a nest of clouds. Yonatan turned his back on the crowd, savoring the expensive cognac he was partial to and contemplating the rare sight when he was joined by another guest.

Annoyed at the distraction, he turned to find the unknown citizen from the land of volcanoes whom he had noticed earlier. The stranger was strikingly clad in a sumptuous black leather jacket and a characteristic soft black robe. He wore the silver sigil of a healer on his lapel, something Yonatan thought rather ostentatious.

The stranger introduced himself and they exchanged ritual toasts to the elders. He dropped a few names, signaling to Yonatan that he was indeed well connected. He implied, delicately, that he was intimate with some of the elders.

"I understand that you, like myself, are a sanctioned re-educator." He swigged some of his expensive scotch and shook his head. "We're going to be busier than ever in the coming days as more citizens are infected by this religionist movement. Even now it is filtering up among our class." The stranger waved a hand at the crowd of partiers reflected in the huge window.

"I have not, myself, noticed an upsurge in business," Yonatan said, temperately.

"And you wouldn't tell me if you did. I know," the other man smiled, "as healers we are committed to keeping our patients' secrets. And this city has always been blessed with the peace that comes from being far from the centers of power.

Annoyed at being relegated to the status of a provincial hick, Yonatan was contemplating a suitably cutting riposte when the stranger said, "These protestors of yours are reportedly riddled with religionists."

"They are not my protestors," Yonatan tried not to sound testy, "but I thought they were just rabid anti-ephemerists."

"One and the same. But the protestors down in their little camp will be taken care of by the authorities. You and I will need to successfully re-educate the people behind them, when they are uncovered."

He shook his head sadly, "A difficult task, correcting the unsanctioned beliefs of the committed religionist."

"I'm usually pretty successful," Yonatan said drily.

"Oh, yes. As am I. Anyway, the Conclave of Elders is very concerned about rising religionism. They will be issuing new directives, especially addressing our disposition of religionists. In the past, in the rare instances when our treatment protocols were unsuccessful, we regretfully turned our patients over to the authorities."

He looked sharply at Yonatan, who nodded.

"An exception will be made for religionists. From now on we will be sanctioned to use a new treatment modality."

"A new treatment modality? You mean there is a new drug?"

"No, actually there is a new tool." The stranger was watching Yonatan, who was for some reason shaken by the other man's tone.

"What kind of tool?" he asked, not really wanting to know. As a student of the mind he had trained himself to interpret unconscious cues. This citizen enjoyed power.

"It's for those cases which would otherwise have to go to re-education camps." The other man's tone was rather jolly. "Fortunately the conclave's scientists have developed a device to assist us. Really a rather crafty gadget." He put his hand into the pocket of his beautiful jacket, which Yonatan now realized with a shudder was made from real animal skin. He opened his fist to reveal a small black ovoid plastic object, about the size and color of a cockroach, with tiny blue lights, like eyes, on either side. It was fastened to a fine chain, presumably to be hung around the neck. A miniscule icon was embossed on one side.

"This is the receiver. The scientists developed this as an outgrowth of their mission to miniaturize weapons. When activated it affects certain brain waves. Within 24 hours the affected patients will commit suicide."

"Suicide?" Yonatan stuttered, not comprehending.

"In 99.9 percent of cases." The other man smiled.

"And the point one percent?"

The other man said with gusto: "Psychopaths. It doesn't work well on them."

He launched into a technical description of the part of the brain that was affected. Yonatan's own brain was reeling.

"How is it activated?" he asked, when the other man wound down.

The other man pulled another item from his pocket, a black box about the size of a matchbox. A button embossed with an icon that matched the one on the receiver was centered on one side.

"You just push the button and it activates the receiver. They are tuned to each other. The receiver works pretty quickly. It must stay in place for a couple hours. Of course, it has to be close to the body of the target, worn as a necklace or in a pocket, for example."

"So if I pushed the button right now, the receiver you are holding in your hand would affect your brain waves and you would commit suicide? Within 24 hours?" Yonatan pointed to the activator button.

"Often it is quicker, but 24 hours is the outside time limit."

"Of course, of course." Yonatan sipped some cognac.

"It's drawback as a weapon is that it must be close to the target. The scientists who developed it were disappointed with its effective range until one of their number realized it would be useful for one-on-one missions."

"Assassinations," Yonatan murmured. "Better than blowing up a school full of children."

The other man looked puzzled.

"Just an historical reference." Yonatan finished his drink.

"When will the C.E. issue this directive?"

"Soon. It will be provided only to sanctioned re-educators, of course. And the treatment is mandatory. It's beauty, of course, is that no suspicions will be aroused against the healer."

He looked at his glass as if surprised it was empty. "Shall we join the others? I could use a refill." He floated off, his long soft robe, so reminiscent of the public images of the elders, billowing slightly.

Yonatan was left staring at his own empty glass.

"I'm a healer," he thought. "Now I am to be an executioner, too."

He could smell his hostess's perfume as she came up behind him, wrapping her arm around his waist. "I see you have been making friends with our very dear friend from the Conclave," she lilted. "He can be so helpful to your career. And his long robe is charming, don't you think."

Yonatan allowed himself to be swept back to the throng. He made unthinking small talk as he worked his way to the door, eager to get out of the flat, into the dark city.

Before he could leave, however, he was accosted by a man he knew as a toady of the city's high administration. "We know you have business dealings with Piet Lem of Grupo Uno," he grunted. "We are anxious to talk with him privately about activities in the Subs." Yonatan felt something slide into his pocket. "Give him this card and have him get in touch."

He hastily felt the object in his pocket. It was just a card.

Could the evening get worse?

Yes, it could.

When Yonatan approached the door of his block of flats, a figure detached from the shadows. It was Beau Lem, Piet's son, very much in Piet's mold, tall, slender and soft footed. He had Piet's quiet, forceful delivery down pat, too.

"Dad sends his respects and wonders if you could give him some assistance," Beau whispered. It was not a request.

"I would be honored," Yonatan was tired of being manipulated, "but he'll have to come to me. Tell him I'll meet him at Sparrow's." Beau demurred but Yonatan was adamant. He suddenly couldn't face an empty flat or a midnight trip to the Subs.

As Yonatan walked the dark streets of the city, he was assimilating, or trying to assimilate, this new view of himself as someone who, when he failed to heal a patient, was required to put into motion a modality which would drive the patient to despair so profound it would inevitably result in self destruction. As a sanctioned re-educator, he had taken an oath to obey the directives of the Conclave of Elders. If they ordered him to utilize this new tool, he would be required to obey. As a student of the mind and emotions, he knew the pain necessary to drive an otherwise healthy mind to such extremes. Only an especially determined citizen could resist his more conventional treatments so he would be using this tool on the brightest, most dedicated of citizens. He had, in his practice, taken some patients to places of deep disorientation and self-doubt then brought them back with their resolve renewed and their thoughts corrected. All such patients were not religionists, either. Some were committed to beliefs that could lead them to challenge the Conclave. If circumstances were slightly different, Arlo Gauss, for example, would be the type he would be called upon to treat. Yonatan did not know Arlo well, but he thought he would be one who would resist, that Yonatan would be forced to send him on a downward spiral of self-loathing and death.

4

Although it seemed an eternity since Yonatan had gone to the party, when he arrived at the House of Blue Leaves, the evening was in full swing. As an intimate of Sparrow's, he was immediately recognized and ushered toward the cafe, a floor below the raucous main club.

The cafe was off a central reception area where house employees of all ages and genders displayed themselves for selection by clients. Doors led to hallways radiating from the foyer where the employees entertained in private rooms. Customers could select anyone available, all employees were clad in togas and the various colors in the hems of the garments indicated the level of service offered by the individual worker: plain white togas were worn by postulants who were limited to providing the four basic modes of sexual pleasure and whose services were the least expensive; blood red indicated Dominex, who were quite expensive and available for sanctioned types of bondage; royal blue was for

Courtesans, the most accomplished and also the most expensive sex workers.

Once inside the cafe, he was surprised, not pleasantly, to see Arlo Gauss himself seated at a table with one of the young postulants.

A small, ugly man with great charm, once seen, never forgotten, Yonatan had only met Arlo on one other occasion, in the company of Piet Lem. His reputation was vast. A large bounty was supposed to reward his recovery by the authorities for numerous political crimes against the citizenry. Yet he seemed to come and go in the city with impunity. His relationship with the famous scientist and criminal Menard Tillman was legendary. Tillman was supposed to have been relegated to the stasis chamber for high crimes but reportedly had escaped. His whereabouts were unknown, except, possibly, to Arlo Gauss. He was also connected somehow to the even more famous scientist, Desmond Elvistine, who had vanished mysteriously on a trip to the Conclave. In short, a citizen perpetually living in the eye of the storm.

He smiled his charming smile at Yonatan and motioned toward an empty seat at his table. Gnomish describes him, Yonatan thought. He was not quite real amid the hard materialists of the New Dispensation.

The postulant took off, happy with a large cash tip, returning with Yonatan's cognac and a glass of tea.

They sat in silence for a while, Arlo seemingly at ease, drinking his tea, Yonatan overwhelmed with the events of the evening. Finally he could stand the quiet no longer and said, "I'm expecting to meet with Piet Lem."

"Good," Arlo said. "Maybe he can tell us what is going on with the protestors."

"The protestors?" Yonatan said sharply then regretted his tone as the other man took notice.

Yonatan opted for a diversion. "I don't quite understand the protestors. To be honest, I never paid much attention to them. I thought they were just misguided citizens with a grudge against ephemerists, whatever they are." Yonatan waved a hand to illustrate his lack of understanding. "Now, I hear a rumor they are some kind of religionists."

"I expect there are religionists among them. Anti-ephemerists and religionists have a similar agenda." Arlo waved to a passing waiter for more tea.

"Perhaps you can explain it to me." When the waiter returned with Arlo's tea, Yonatan ordered a dish of sweetmeats and more cognac. He had a feeling Arlo was going to become technical. He would start out by saying, it's simple, and it wouldn't be.

"It's simple," Arlo said. "Uninformed citizens have come to view the theoretical sciences, what they call deep science, as dangerous. They term scientists who practice deep science ephemerists because their initial work is speculative, ephemeral. If it remained pure thought, it would not be a problem, but, in their view, all too often, the speculation leads to terrifying real occurrences. For example, the abolishing of countries and the institution of centralized direction under the Conclave of Elders were based on extensive speculative writings. After the plague, the initial founders of the Conclave used the writings as a blueprint for action. Or the opening of a portal to another universe. That was based on the theoretical physics of deep scientists such as Tillman and

Desmond Elvistine."

"I don't know why they are worried about the portal. Nothing ever came of it." Yonatan interrupted.

"Not yet. They are worried that something bad might happen if the scientists keep messing around with it." Arlo shook his head dismissively, started to comment, then returned to topic.

"The religionists' agenda, on the other hand, is opposed to deep science because religion depends on belief in things—beings, events—that are not conducive of proof in a scientific sense. As deep scientists conduct more and more experiments and make discoveries that do not support their beliefs, they feel their followers will lose their ability to believe in the unbelievable.

"The irony is, of course, that religionists themselves are the ultimate ephemerists. Their beliefs are pure speculation."

"And that is just what you do, Healer Belasco, as a re-educator. You change citizens' beliefs."

Yonatan didn't care for his tone. Nettled, he said, "No, I don't always change their beliefs, per se. Citizens are entitled to believe anything they desire. When they are willing to act on their beliefs in a way that endangers themselves or other citizens, that willingness must be addressed. Often my role is merely pointing out the harmful result of their actions to effect the desired outcome, namely to improve their behavior. Some people are mentally ill, then they are put under restraint and special drugs are called for."

"And," Yonatan sighed, "Some people like to

work their emotions extra hard. They become excitable, violent. They require special services." He had started to say special modalities then stopped himself when a vision of the black suicide machine arose. He thought he might come to hate that word.

He continued, "After all, a belief is just a thought. With the appropriate treatment, thoughts can be disrupted."

"Not a pleasant experience, I imagine," Arlo said.

"Better than a re-education camp."

"Have you been inside a re-education camp? As a visitor, I mean." Arlo asked curiously. Few citizens had.

"Yes." Yonatan glanced at the door, relieved to see Piet Lem approaching. "Let's change the subject."

Piet Lem folded himself neatly into a chair and fist bumped the two men. His usual stoic calm looked forced, and he smiled grimly when Sparrow waddled over with a tray and a bottle of Piet's favorite brandy.

They sat in polite silence for a few minutes then formally toasted the elders.

Piet said to Yonatan, "I need you."

Yonatan said, "I was at a party tonight." He named the host and Piet merely nodded impatiently. He knew Yonatan was from an old, aristocratic family.

"One of the guests gave me this." He handed Piet the card that had been slipped into his pocket. Piet looked at it then at Yonatan.

"They asked that you get in touch."

Piet swore. "Do you know what they want?"

"No."

Yonatan then briefly recounted his conversation with his fellow healer at the party and described the item he claimed would be sanctioned for unrepentant religionists.

"Another item from the wonderful people in the C.E.'s secret labs." Arlo commented. He started to mention to Piet his need for assistance getting to Deep Cove, but, before they could continue the conversation, Beau hurried in from the foyer where he been chatting with some of Sparrow's young employees. A harried looking waiter followed him and whispered in Sparrow's ear, prompting him to look at his wrist comm.

Their host whistled then looked around the table with keen curiosity.

"There's been a huge explosion," he said."

Piet flinched and grasped Sparrow's fat wrist. "In the Subs?" he said.

"In the protestors' camp."

They all spoke at once.

"Were many citizens hurt?

"A fusion device?"

"Where exactly in the protestors' camp." This last question was from Arlo.

Sparrow held up a hand. "There is not a lot of information. The data I have is not from the authorities so it could be questionable."

"As would be any data from the authorities," Yonatan said.

Sparrow frowned, "According to my sources, many people were killed by an old fashioned exploding bomb. People are claiming it came from the sky."

This last statement brought further concern among the men; they all remembered stories of the plague from the sky.

As the evening progressed, Sparrow's employees brought in a steady stream of updates. The city authorities and civil defense troops were out in force, every corner had a functionary with a weapon of some kind.

Loudspeakers announced that the city was on lockdown and a full curfew was in force. High intensity lamps flooded the city with light, erasing shadows in which those unfortunates without ID or recourse to the Subs could hide. Citizens found on the streets without identification badges were being herded into holding pens and held under close watch.

Yonatan, who was a member of the city's volunteer emergency medical team, left to attend the injured. He promised to send information when he had a chance but warned them it might be a long time depending on the number of wounded and the extent of their injuries.

Rumors abounded, but hard intel was scarce.

Arlo decided to take a chance on the streets in an attempt to get back to the flat. He planned to gather a few items and take refuge in the Subs with Piet.

Piet and Beau were anxious to return to the Subs.

5

In Deep Cove, Rick was stretched out in a comfortable chair on the topmost terrace of his villa from which he could see the open countryside, a convenient glass of tea placed nearby by Linnet. Rick's villa was designed in the local style consisting of one and two story buildings surrounding a central courtyard surmounted by rooftop terraces at different levels. The sea was behind him, and he could hear the soothing surf.

Below him and out of sight, his wife, Ilsa, and Linnet chatted together on the large terrace outside the kitchen. Jordi Petrie, who was being nursed by Linnet as he recovered from a shotgun blast, was asleep in his room. Ana, Colt's crazy wife, was working feverishly on her computer and Teegan, Jordi's wife, was off somewhere in Rick's aircar. Teegan and Jordi were not getting along, and Rick was happy to have her out of the way because she seemed like someone who was born to cause trouble. Colt, typically, had disappeared. Rick knew he was still

31

worried about Ana's safety, but they were all determined to return to the city the next day. Rick was already enjoying the feeling of being back in control of his own home.

A big feral cat that Ilsa insisted on feeding lazed in one corner, half asleep and occasionally licking a paw. Its contentment mirrored Rick's feelings. With all his unwelcome guests finally gone, and the authorities apparently unaware of the brief explosion of violence and death unleashed by Irene Thorne, he and Ilsa could get back to their normal placid existence. The healers had assured him that his heart was in great shape for a man of his age—Linnet had taken wonderful care of him after his coronary—and her husband Oren was proving a valuable addition to the household.

With youthful resilience, Oren and Linnet had recovered from being used in Irene's scheme to produce a superbaby with Irene's eggs and Elvistine's brilliant DNA, using Linnet, who was fertile, as a surrogate.

Oren came onto the terrace and flopped at his feet. He was a stocky countryman, not too bright, but a wonderful mechanic and tireless worker. Now he seemed restless; Rick had been a teacher long enough to recognize the symptoms. The younger man wanted to discuss something. Rick let the silence unwind.

"It's nice out here," Oren finally said. "I never seen the sea before. Is it true there are monsters in the water?"

"I've never seen one myself but the fishermen tell stories, although they never seem to catch anything but a few fish. Ilsa and I don't go in the water, though."

"Do they eat the fish?" Oren said, momentarily distracted. When Rick nodded, he grimaced. More silence as Oren poured himself another cup of tea. Finally he said, "Linnet says Ilsa is fertile."

"Yes."

"Linnet is too."

"I know, Ilsa told me."

"I thought she would. She and Linnet are getting along good."

Oren jumped up and turned to gaze at the ocean, which had assumed a deep purple color.

"Ilsa has not been a surrogate?" he said softly.

"No."

"She doesn't want to do it?" Oren continued looking out at the water.

This was a sensitive topic and none of Oren's business, but Rick said, "We don't want her to do it." He stressed the we.

"You could have had children yourselves."

"We could, but we would want to raise them ourselves."

"Oh." Oren said neutrally. "That could cause some problems."

Rick sighed. "It would cause lots of problems, even in a backwater like this. The local authorities would insist the children be placed in a crèche and people would not leave Ilsa alone."

"They would want her to be a surrogate for them like Irene Thorne wanted for Linnet and that professor."

"Professor Elvistine, yes. Most people would not perpetrate a kidnapping, as Irene did." Rick and Oren both remembered the scene that had played out on the same veranda where they were sitting. When an armed Irene Thorne and her goon had descended by helicopter demanding to be led to Elvistine so his sperm could impregnate Irene's eggs, which would then be implanted in Linnet. Colt and Chandler Besdine had killed them.

Rick said, "But that isn't a problem for you and Linnet. You could return to the community and have children there. Linnet said she has several brothers and sisters and they were raised by her parents."

"I have brothers, myself, and we were raised by our parents. But that doesn't happen any more. The patriarchs only did that until they got enough people to support the community. Nowadays when the girl is fertile, the couple gets to keep the first child and it is raised in the community crèche. Later children are raised in crèches outside the community."

"Then when they grow up they are returned to the community?" Rick was puzzled by Oren's remarks.

"No, I don't think so. I don't know where they go. The community can only support so many people."

"Why don't they just sterilize the girls after they have the first child, saving themselves the trouble of providing medical care and supporting the crèches."

"I don't think they can do that, sterilize people."

Rick didn't say so, but he knew they could. He assumed the community elders were selling the babies.

"Linnet and me, we don't want to go back to the community anyway," Oren said. "She likes it here. Besides, like you, I want to raise my own children."

"You can stay here as long as you like," Rick said, thinking that would end the discussion for the moment. He knew Linnet's fertility and capacity to surrogate presented problems for the young couple and expected more conversations while they decided what to do. Under the New Dispensation, keeping a child at home was nearly impossible.

Rick relaxed too soon. Oren had something else on his mind.

"Rick, you've had a lot of experience and you know a lot of stuff."

Bemused, Rick was once again silent.

"Have you ever heard of the Man in the Sky?" Oren spoke very quietly, glancing around as though looking for invisible ears.

"The Man in the Sky?" Rick tried to keep his voice steady, but he was shaken.

"Yes. They say he can do things for you, if you ask."

"Where did you hear about this sky man?" Rick could hardly keep his voice steady.

"We talked about him in the community, secretly. A special citizen, the Sojourner he is called, teaches us about the Man."

"That's religionism, you know, Oren. And talking about the Man in the Sky is particularly unsanctioned. The Conclave is extremely hard on citizens who discuss him."

"I know, but that's because they are his enemy." Rick heard the conviction in his voice.

"But he isn't religionist, not really." Oren went on. "The Sojourner says religionism is about believing in beings that don't exist. The old people were religionists, but, when the plague came, it didn't help them. But the Man in the Sky is different. He's real."

"Then why didn't he help the people when the

plague came?"

"The Sojourner explained that. Those people were not special, they were not his people. The ones who survived were special."

"I see," Rick said.

"And once the Conclave is destroyed, the Man in the Sky will come to the world and make it like it was even before the times of the old people, like a garden."

"And is the Man in the Sky going to destroy the Conclave?" Rick asked, rhetorically, because he knew where this was headed.

"Oh, no," Oren assured him. "The Man in the Sky is good. Besides we citizens have to destroy the Conclave for him, to show we are worthy."

"Worthy of the garden?" Rick said softly.

"Yes." Oren smiled. "In the garden Linnet and I was can have all the children we want."

"Have you discussed this with Linnet?"

He frowned and looked sad. "Yes, but she doesn't like to discuss it. She doesn't understand that it isn't religionism. She doesn't believe the Sojourner. She says he is just a man. But she won't say anything to anyone."

"Just be careful who you discuss this with." Rick said.

Oren grinned happily. "Oh, I will Rick. But I know I can trust you."

The discussion terminated when Ilsa came onto the terrace with a carafe of honey wine and small dishes of soy cheese and nuts.

Linnet followed shortly with the rest of the evening meal and the topic was dropped.

Later, Rick and Ilsa were taking a leisurely walk on the beach behind the villa. Oren and Linnet were in the kitchen, cleaning up after the evening meal. Rick could hear them laughing.

As they followed the stone steps down to the sand, Ilsa chattered about her relief that their houseguests would be leaving the next day. She was surprised when Rick took another path than usual, turning away from the lights of the village. Ilsa followed with some trepidation as they shortly reached an open space where the likelihood of being overheard was minimal.

Rick kissed Ilsa, a nice, long, loving kiss. They both still enjoyed each other.

"We've got a problem," he said.

"Yes, or maybe two problems." Ilsa took his hand to her lips and kissed his knuckles. "You go first."

"I had a talk with Oren this afternoon. We've got to get rid of him and Linnet. Oren has become a religionist."

"He's a young man," Ilsa pointed out. "They go through phases."

"I don't think this is a phase. He mentioned the Man in the Sky."

Ilsa looked shocked, "Oh, that's bad. They are reputed to be the worst kind of fanatics. I thought they wiped that group out."

"Apparently not."

"Oh, Rick," Ilsa held him tightly. "I'm terrified. If they find out about him and he's living here, that we're harboring him, they'll send us all to re-education camp. Or worse."

He held her for a while. There was nothing to say.

Finally she said, "And my problem just makes it worse. Linnet's pregnant."

"Does Oren know yet?"

"No, it's still early. I urged her not to say anything hoping that, because she is young, she would miscarry."

"Do whatever you can to keep her from telling him."

They stood for a long time holding each other. They had left the city to seek sanctuary and peace away from gossip and ill speaking. Now their refuge was facing real dangers.

6

Colt and Jordi were sick of living in a small village and found the household at the villa tiresome. They especially disliked Oren, who had developed a kind of hero worship of Colt, something Colt found irritating. He had been a famous cage fighter and had grown sick of the fans and the mindless adulation that the C.E. encouraged. He had gone so far as to change his name, adopting Ana's when they entered their sanctioned relationship. Colt was also worried about Jordi, who seemed increasingly irrational. Colt wanted to get him back to the city where Yonatan Belasco could take a look at him.

Now they were drinking vodka at one of the little open-air cafes on the beach, glad to get away from the tensions back at the villa. Jordi had not fully recovered physically but a couple hours of rustic gossip were just what he needed.

Around the bar, a group of locals were retelling a story about one of the giant eight-legged sea spiders that someone claimed to have glimpsed.

Before Colt and Jordi could ask any questions about the eight-legs, there was an interruption. The video over the bar had been replaying an old semifinal game between two Navy lacrosse teams when the general alert logo had appeared. The bartender immediately turned up the volume. The pleasant, vaguely exotic, female voice used for all general alerts came on the air.

"Until further notice, all unnecessary access to and egress from the city is now forbidden as a result of unsanctioned violence. Roadblocks have been established on all major roads and the army will be patrolling a perimeter of one klick around the city. Violators attempting to cross the perimeter or to breach the roadblocks will be shot on sight."

The report ended with the obligatory Elders' Hymn then returned to the lacrosse match.

Various comms flashed around the room as customers tried to contact citizens in or near the city for information. Eventually a rather garbled report of an explosion with many casualties came through. Although the report did not specifically refer to the protestors' camp, it referenced the district where Colt and Jordi knew the camp was located. Of more concern to all was a vague report that the explosion was a result of something coming from the sky. Everyone knew that the plague, which had almost completely wiped out the inhabitants of the planet, had reportedly come from the sky.

Several ex-military customers cautioned against panic. They said they knew the army had explosive missiles that could be shot from big guns and would appear to come from above. Everyone knew that nothing larger than an unmanned satellite could actually fly.

Why the Conclave, which controlled all the military forces, would be shooting missiles into the city was the question of the moment. The concept was frightening but preferable to the prospect of another plague, which would undoubtedly wipe out life on the planet. Most assumed it was another fruitless religionist-inspired uprising.

"Armageddon," Jordi whispered to Colt, grinning.

Colt wanted to sock him.

When they reached the villa, their attention was claimed by the flash of a small light on the highest terrace at the front of the residence. They could see Ilsa leaning over the parapet, holding a finger in front of her mouth for silence, and gesturing them toward the side of the building where the terrace was accessible via an external staircase. They assumed they would ascend to the roof, but, instead, she was waiting at the bottom of the staircase. Wrapped in a long dark robe, they could barely see her. Her long hair was blowing wildly in the wind. Clearly distraught, she gripped their arms with icy hands and dragged them toward the beach.

Instead of stopping on the shore, she led them toward a circle of large bushes that offered some protection from the winds off the water and was mostly used as an outdoor privy for people having picnics on the beach. Once inside, Ilsa sighed. They could tell from her voice that she had been crying.

"Come in here," she whispered. "Sound carries by

the water."

Jordi slipped off his jacket and draped it around her. "I'm so terrified." She whispered. "You've got to help us." She whispered an account of Oren's belief in the Man in the Sky and told them about Linnet's pregnancy. "This is too much for Rick. He'll have another heart attack. And, if the authorities find out about Oren, they will send us all to re-education camps or to the stasis chambers." She burst into tears and Jordi held her close. Some of her terror seemed to infect him.

"What do you want us to do?" Colt whispered.

"You've got to get Oren away from us. Make him go to the city or back to his community. If he won't go, you will have to kill him. Use your fusion pistol."

"What about Linnet?"

Ilsa cried harder. "She will have to go with him. I'll miss her. She's a wonderful person, but she cherishes him. Oren told Rick she wasn't a follower of the religion. Maybe we could talk to her tomorrow, explain the danger he poses. Get her to help us."

As they walked back to the villa, through the implacable darkness, Colt found himself taking on the mood of the night. He adored and trusted Ana but she kept secrets from him. He had thought he could trust Linnet, the little country mouse, as Sparrow had called her. Colt had saved her life twice. Yet, since she had rejoined Oren, he was no longer sure of her allegiance. He thought he could trust Jordi, who was like a brother, although if Jordi had to choose between Colt and Teegan, he would probably choose his wife just as Colt would likely choose Ana. And Jordi was becoming unstable.

7

"Armageddon!" Colt Bede leaped into the air and savagely kicked at one of the defenseless little pine trees that were sprinkled around the rocky shore. How he hated those words from the old times, old religions. They were probably unsanctioned, illegal, and what did Ana know about Armageddon anyway.

She was brilliant but she was a mathematician, not an historian. She had claimed her mentor had disappeared from his sickbed through an interdimensional portal; an action that she claimed had initiated Armageddon—the end of the world. The story made no sense to Colt, and Ana remained unwilling to talk to anyone, even him, about what had happened to Desmond Elvistine.

"You better not let anyone hear you use that word," Teegan Petrie had emerged from the villa and thrown a backpack into the aircar that waited to take them back to the city.

"You'll be sent to a re-education camp for sure."

She glanced behind her to see who was nearby,

and seeing no one, pointed to her watch. Colt nodded.

A small group emerged from the villa and joined them. Jordi was leaning on Oren. He was healed from his injuries—fortunately his assailant had shot him with a conventional weapon rather than a fusion pistol—but he was pale and thin, still weak. The visit to the village the previous night had exhausted him. And his friends were worried that his mental health was deteriorating.

Oren helped Jordi into the aircar, then fist bumped Colt.

"Be careful," he said. Oren's wife, Linnet, gave Colt a little pat on the arm. She was crying, worried about them in the city and sad that they were leaving. Colt had saved her from starving to death on the streets of the city. She and Oren had decided to stay behind with Rick and Ilsa, the owners of the villa in Deep Cove, while they decided where to settle down.

Despite the lockdown, the two couples were adamant they must return to the city. They explained to Rick and the others that the lockdown was likely to be temporary and, anyway, they could find a way into the city through the Subs. Although they didn't mention it, they were all city dwellers and anxious to return there after the boredom of the village. Colt was anxious to put Jordi under Yonatan's care.

Rick and Ilsa also came out to say goodbye. Rick had not wanted any of their company from the beginning and after the shocking events of the past weeks; he was more than pleased to see them go. They had intruded in his and Ilsa's little haven by the sea, brought death and misery, and more important, possible attention from the authorities.

Oren and Linnet would have to go, too, Rick thought sadly. Oren, having grown up on a communal farm, was used to hard work, and Linnet had proved to be a competent and compassionate nurse for Rick after his heart attack and a gentle companion for Ilsa, who was too sensitive and fastidious to do nursing or heavy housework. But they were religionists, and he would have to find a way to get rid of them.

Thankfully, Rick thought, Piet Lem and his son Beau had taken off immediately after the shooting, commandeering Irene's helicopter. Piet and Beau were anxious to get back to the city, where they felt safe and had business. Mercifully they had taken Chandler Besdine with them.

Rick was still troubled by Chandler's presence at the villa. Piet Lem, as head of Grupo Uno, was just a legitimate crook but Chandler was mysterious, his agendas unknown. Rick remembered teaching him at the university. He was brilliant and his connection to the Conclave of Elders was impeccable, a connection which would trouble any right-thinking citizen of the New Dispensation most of whom sought to avoid coming to the attention of that august body. Also he had shown a distressing attachment to the traitor, Tillman.

Thanks be to the elders, they were leaving at last, Rick thought.

Ana, Colt's wife, was the last to join the group by the aircar. She held a tablet on which she had been compulsively scribbling equations for days. She had not slept and her hair was uncombed. She gave Rick a phantom kiss on the cheek and briefly hugged Ilsa, who tried not to recoil. Ana had not been showering, either.

Teegan and Jordi were already in the aircar, the tension between them obvious from their postures. Colt's nod to Ana was perfunctory as he opened the door for her and started the controls. He hoped she would not start crying. Her nerves were shot and she had been working to exhaustion pursuant to one of Elvistine's cockamamie theories.

Although glad to see them whoosh out of sight as the aircar rose two feet above the ground and headed toward the city, Rick didn't envy them the tension-filled journey. Everyone would be looking at the scenery; no one would be seeing it.

8

Barely five minutes after the aircar carrying Colt, Ana, Teegan, and Jordi left the village of Deep Cove, as they were passing through the village where Elvistine had disappeared, Teegan reached forward and touched the power icon.

As the vehicle floated gently to the ground, Teegan said, "I'm not going anywhere in this aircar until Ana takes a shower and puts her clothes through a sanitizer. If I'd known how bad she reeked back at Rick's, I would have said something then." Teegan opened the vehicle's door and hurried outside, taking shelter under a scrubby tree.

"I don't know if it's safe to get out here," Ana said. "They might recognize me."

Dr. Elvistine had been badly injured when his aircar was attacked by bandits but had escaped when a rival group showed up to fight for the valuable vehicle. He had managed to walk to a nearby inn from which he had contacted Ana, who rushed to his side. Although he had refused to see a local healer, when he became unconscious, they had transferred him to the regional clinic in this village. Ana had stayed with him while Colt went on to Deep Cove to liaise with the rest of their company.

Ana had claimed to the people in Deep Cove that the professor had managed to activate an interdimensional portal through which he had left the clinic. Fallout from the activation had caused an explosion and fire, which local authorities had used to explain the complete disappearance of the patient.

"What difference would it make if they did recognize you?" Teegan asked. "They thought your father died in an explosion. They don't know he opened an interdimensional portal." She giggled.

She was referring to the fact that, to avoid attracting attention, Ana and Colt had admitted the noted scientist to the clinic using Ana's father's name. And alluding to the hope that no one knew about the interdimensional portal comment except those who had been present. News videos merely reported that the noted deep scientist had died of a heart attack and been cremated.

"Maybe Teegan's right," Colt coaxed Ana. "The clinic staff probably have no contact with the bathhouse. No one will see you."

"They are all watching all the time anyway," Jordi said in a harsh whisper. He glanced covertly upward, "They have eyes everywhere, mutant birds, flying spiders with eyes."

They all looked at him concerned, but he did not see their glances. He was sitting with his eyes tightly closed.

Teegan shook her head at Colt as he started to reach for her husband, to try to bring him back.

Teegan returned to the aircar and they all followed her, Jordi slouching along behind, head hanging. She punched the icon for the bathhouse.

"You don't think there will be a problem, do you?" Ana grabbed her husband's arm. He shrugged it off, watching Jordi.

The clinic was a large multistory building with an adjacent helipad; it had been built to serve an extensive, sparsely populated area. The bathhouse was on a side street behind the main clinic building so the aircar zipped past the clinic front with its prominent green cross and turned down a side street before descending and stopping before a squat structure displaying the blue teardrop shape that denoted water. Water alone was no longer the choice for personal cleanliness, most citizens used sonic showers, but the icon was still used. For aesthetic reasons, bathhouses would offer a small pool of fragrant fluid in which clients could immerse themselves. The aircar paused before the door of the bathhouse and dropped to allow Ana and Teegan to exit.

Across the street from the bathhouse, a small park had been built at the rear of the clinic. The street and park were mostly empty. A few citizens wearing hospital garb wandered among the statues of Elders that decorated the area. They seemed uninterested in the aircar but Colt saw a man wearing the robe of a healer give it a sharp look.

"Go with Ana and make sure she gets taken care of," Colt said to Teegan. "We're going to get the aircar out of sight."

Teegan nodded and took Ana's arm and led her into the bathhouse.

"Get yourself a massage or something," Jordi

encouraged his wife, handing her some cash tokens. His strange mood seemed to have disappeared.

Colt watched, interested in how she would respond. She put a finger to her lips, kissed it, and blew the kiss in Jordi's direction. It was a nice gesture. She winked at Colt then pulled Ana through the door of the bathhouse. Colt frowned. He hated duplicity.

Colt and Jordi tucked the aircar behind the bathhouse where it was in the shadow cast by a large chemical tank. Then they wandered over to the little park.

Jordi was shaky and thin from his ordeal. Piet Lem had been able to find a healer who would not report a gunshot to the authorities, but they had not been able to provide the professional care Jordi had needed. The clinic seemed too public, and he had been too badly injured to transport to the Subs. They had been forced to rely on the unsanctioned healer and Linnet's care. She seemed to have a natural talent for nursing.

Colt left Jordi on a bench where he could contemplate a statuary group representing the elders, depicted in their long white robes, patting the heads of a group of stoic children. Jordi, who was a gifted, if untrained, artist, contented himself with contemplating the overall lack of expertise displayed by the sculptor. Obviously the local authorities had not been able to afford a university-trained artist. Jordi wondered who the sculptor had used for models; the elders' expressions could be described as mindless, even moronic.

Meanwhile Colt wandered aimlessly along the paths that radiated from the central group, strolling among the patients, eventually finding himself close to the healer he had noticed earlier.

The amber worry beads the healer was fondling prompted the memory of Elvistine, who was cared for by this large, pompous citizen. Colt wondered if the healer knew what happened to Elvistine.

He heard the healer say, "Citizen Bede, isn't it. I thought I recognized you,"

At this angle, Jordi's bench was hidden from view by the sculptural group.

The two men fist bumped.

The healer looked much like he had the last time Colt had seen him. At that time, he had been busy and had little time to chat. Colt hoped the same was true today. He wanted to get the business over with.

"I thought I saw your wife go into the bathhouse," he said.

"Yes, we were traveling to the city and my wife had a slight accident. She spilled a sweet drink on her lap and insisted she couldn't continue traveling without a shower and putting her clothes in a sanitizer."

"I see. Good story." The healer fiddled with his worry beads and looked away.

"The accident that happened to your father-in-law was most regrettable." He swung the beads in a little arc. Colt wondered if he used hypnosis in his practice.

"The authorities were never able to determine what caused the fire," he murmured.

"No." Colt had the same problem.

"Also, they were quite puzzled by the lack of body parts. The explosion and fire didn't seem extreme enough to cause complete disintegration, similar to that caused by a fusion pistol, for example."

"I wouldn't know anything about that," Colt said.

He rocked on his arches and flexed, hoping to

communicate his cluelessness about practically everything.

"Your wife's behavior was unusual." The citizen continued staring across the small park.

"She was really upset," Colt said.

"You expect that," the healer said, "when a family member dies, especially in a freak accident. But I was more struck by the way she seemed, you know, afraid."

"Afraid?"

"I would say terrified was the word."

"She seemed in shock to me," Colt said, honestly.

"Oh, that too. But I've had a lot of experience. I was in the militia for a few years. I've seen terror." He paused. "She was terrified. Until the authorities arrived. Then she seemed to calm down."

"She probably knew the authorities would take care of things," Colt said.

"She's high strung," he continued. "I'm trying to take care of her."

"I know." The citizen flipped his worry beads around his wrist and slipped back into the clinic.

Jordi was still sitting gazing at the central group of statuary, his long legs stretched out in front of him. Colt's backpack rested on the bench. When Colt kicked the bottom of Jordi's boot, he came out of his reverie.

"Those may be the worst looking images of elders that I've seen," he said. "The kids are badly rendered, too. The sculptor should be disappeared."

Ignoring this artistic criticism, Colt picked up his backpack.

"Ana and Teegan should be done by now."

Jordi slowly stood up and turned around to face the bathhouse.

"I don't see them," he said.

"No." Colt hurried impatiently toward the bathhouse with Jordi walking slowly behind.

"Teegan always takes forever in the ladies room." Jordi tried to suppress the memory of a dead digger with a chopstick in his throat. The professional snitch had died while Teegan was in a ladies room. Jordi ran his fingers through his hair as if to smooth down his chaotic thoughts.

"I don't see the aircar, either," he added.

"It's in the shadow cast by the outbuilding."

Colt hurried across the street and entered the bathhouse while Jordi scrambled around the side of the building to check on their vehicle.

Inside the bathhouse, the attendant glanced up at him.

"Your wife and her friend left a few minutes ago," she smiled. "They probably went into the gift shop next door for some of our special bath salts."

Before Colt could respond, Jordi hurried through the door behind him.

"Colt," he was breathing hard, "the aircar is gone."

9

Rick watched indifferently as two figures came into view on the path that led to the villa. At first he took them for neighbors or tourists heading for the beach since they were carrying backpacks, but as they came closer, he realized with consternation that they were neither. Colt's light blonde hair and smooth movements were unmistakable; the tall man leaning heavily against him had to be Jordi.

Rick jumped up, scaring the cat, which leapt onto the low parapet and ran away. Rick envied it.

He slowly made his way down to the open doorway, watching as the two men entered the courtyard. Obviously exhausted, Jordi sank down in a chair and threw his backpack on the ground. He was crying loudly, repeating, "She's left me. I know she's left me."

Colt fist bumped Rick and nodded in greeting.

"Has there been an accident?" Rick looked at Jordi.

"Do you have a homing device on the aircar?"

Colt asked.

"Yes, but it is operated from the vehicle, not from here. When you reach the end of your trip, you can send it home empty. It's capable of being called from here but we never needed that function so we never enabled it."

Having heard voices, Ilsa and Linnet joined the men in the courtyard. Ilsa, who had not regained her equilibrium following the disruptions, looked scared, but Linnet immediately hurried over to Jordi and felt his neck.

"We need to get him out of the sun," she said. "You two take him to the guest room where he can rest, and I'll get something for him to drink. He's dehydrated." She looked around the courtyard. "Where are Ana and Teegan?" she asked.

As they got Jordi settled in the guest room, Colt narrated the events from their departure to their discovery of the missing aircar.

Jordi continued crying until Linnet came in with a glass of tea and helped him drink it. The attention seemed to calm him.

"Let's go away and let Jordi rest," she said, leading them upstairs on to the broad terrace at the back of the house.

"Do you think they were kidnapped? Isn't this what you were worried about when you fled the city originally, that someone was threatening Ana? Do you want to contact the authorities?" Rick asked.

"We don't want to contact the authorities," Colt said quickly. "They may have gone off on their own. I had taken my backpack with me, but Jordi had left his in the aircar. When we went to look for the vehicle, his backpack was on the ground. I don't think a third party would have taken the aircar."

"Do you think Teegan instigated the diversion to the bathhouse?" Linnet asked. She didn't care for Teegan.

Colt didn't respond to this provocation. He threw himself into a chair and sipped some tea. He didn't know whether he could trust Rick, but he quickly decided he would take a chance.

"Just before Irene and her goon, Pelham, arrived in the helicopter, I had been having a conversation with Teegan. She said she was leaving Jordi for a citizen named Arlo Gauss."

"I could see she and Jordi were having problems," Ilsa murmured.

"I'm worried about Jordi's mental state," Linnet said.

"So you think she was rushing to this Arlo citizen and dumped you and Jordi. Maybe she thought Jordi might make a scene, try to stop her leaving, if you went into city." Rick said.

"Then why take Ana? She could easily have left while Ana was in the spa and gone in the aircar by herself," Linnet pointed out.

"I don't know. Ana was anxious to get back to the city, to the institute, and more importantly, to Elvistine's office. She said she wanted to see if he had returned there through the portal, or, if not, she wanted to look at his personal notes to determine how he controlled the portal," Colt prevaricated. He did not mention his conversation with the healer.

Ilsa said, "I would be terrified if someone opened an interdimensional portal in front of me."

"This whole interdimensional portal idea sounds far-fetched to me," Rick said. "I am not a deep scientist, but it seems more likely to me that Ana, or someone else, merely used a fusion pistol on Elvistine then started a fire as a cover."

"I am sure that didn't happen," Colt lied. "I believe Ana told us exactly what she saw." Colt controlled his urge to coldcock Rick. "And she had no reason to get rid of Elvistine. He was her mentor and close friend."

"That leads us back to Teegan or some unidentified third party, or Teegan and some unidentified third party." Rick said.

"Arlo," Colt said grimly.

"If you say so. I never met the citizen."

Colt felt a little shiver of suspicion. Arlo was memorable.

"He was in the Marketing and Propaganda Program at university. That was your department, wasn't it?"

"Well, yes. But I cannot place a student named Arlo. What was his second name?" Colt noticed that Ilsa had begun to efface herself when the topic of Arlo emerged. She was drifting toward the door to the kitchen.

"What about you, Ilsa? Do you remember Arlo Gauss?" He said it loud enough that she couldn't pretend not to hear.

She stopped and turned, her beautiful eyes staring into the distance. "I . . . I . . . I think I remember him. He was short and dark, not a very attractive person. You remember, darling," she turned her gaze on Rick, "he made a terrible scene at the party for the new Philosophy of Sanctions instructor and then he got in a lot of trouble and disappeared."

"I remember him now," Rick stroked his jaw

thoughtfully. "He was a brilliant student but he left school before he was in any of my classes. I just didn't recognize the name."

Was Rick lying just for the hell of it, or did he have something to hide, Colt wondered. Everyone remembered Arlo, but wise people often distanced themselves from him.

10

Towards morning, Piet Lem and Beau decided to leave Sparrow's. They needed to get back to the Subs.

Piet urged Beau to hurry. "We probably have time to reach the Subs if we go now while the streets are still chaotic." They thanked Sparrow for his hospitality and left the building through a side door used by employees.

"Have you been through something like this?" Beau asked his father, as they walked purposefully toward the entrance to the Subs.

"Once or twice," Piet answered. "Pull your ID badge out of your shirt so it is visible," he said, hoping no one would scrutinize the counterfeits too closely.

"Don't run," he added. "Anyone in their right mind would be hurrying for cover, but, if you start running, they will shoot you."

They shortly reached the access point, a door hidden behind a large air-handling unit. Once through the door, they both relaxed slightly.

"Do you think they will know about this entrance?" Beau asked. Piet had explained that the authorities would soon be blocking known access points to the Subs and eventually making sweeps downside.

"I don't know. We're not on those kinds of terms. But usually they don't rush down to the Subs because they know we don't encourage religionists. At least not the violent kind." They both grinned because, as Osirans, they were religionists themselves.

This entrance was one of the usual sort, a long narrow corridor, trending vaguely downward into darkness. Because it was used frequently, someone had stuck small very weak lights at intervals near the floor.

Suddenly Piet noticed one of the lights in the distance blink as though someone had walked in front of it. He froze and put a hand on Beau's arm, stopping him, then pulled the small pistol he carried in his boot. He felt Beau lean forward and pull his own weapon.

From the other end of the corridor, a very young voice said, "identify yourself," sounding scared.

"I would say the same to you, citizen," Piet replied. "We're armed."

"Piet Lem. Is that you?" The other one identified himself as one of the novice members of Grupo Uno.

"I know him," Beau whispered to his father.

The shaky young voice continued, "We were told to watch the entrances, hoping to stop you before you went to your trailer."

As he got nearer, Piet turned on the flashlight he always carried and concentrated the small light in the kid's face, blinding him.

"It's him," Beau said. "What's going on?"

"Beau," the kid said. "There are people with guns waiting for you guys at the trailer."

"What?" Beau sounded stunned.

"We don't know them. They are wearing military type uniforms but no one recognizes their insignia. And each one has a bandolier with several fusion grenades." He sounded impressed. Fusion weapons, guns and grenades, were fabulously expensive and even elite military and civil defense units would not issue one to every member.

They had reached the end of the corridor where a door opened to the Subs. The kid explained that he didn't have much more information. He had not seen the people himself and was acting on orders from one of Piet's chief lieutenants.

"Have him meet us." Piet ordered, designating a hidden cubbyhole known only to his senior people.

"Will do." The kid disappeared into the shadows of the Subs in a way that Piet thoroughly approved.

"I hope Rowan's okay," Beau said. They had slapped a patch on her and left her asleep in the trailer until Yonatan could administer his drugs.

"I hope so, too. If she is harmed, we won't find out why Irene was spying on us."

Before they got too far into the Subs where comm frequencies would not work, Piet placed a call to the citizen whose name appeared on the card Yonatan had given him. Apparently the number was private because the personage answered the comm herself. She wanted to meet with Piet immediately. She directed him to a café near the center of the city. Piet directed Beau to proceed to the cubbyhole, keep an eye peeled, and stay there until he returned.

The citizen was there before him, seated at a central table. Several figures stood around the edges of the small room, remaining in the shadows. Rising, she held out her plump hand for a fist bump and seated herself, then pausing, as if deciding, before gesturing for Piet to be seated. They sat in silence. Except for the gravity of the situation, Piet would have gawked, maybe even laughed, at the small dumpy citizen seated with a cup of tea before her. The grey hair was untidy and she was wearing a baggy dress with small flowers that reminded him of Sparrow's usual outfits. When she called for another cup of tea, her voice was squeaky, yet warm, like a teacher in a crèche for babies. She had a slight accent he could not place. Really, he thought, with disquiet, there are more and more foreigners in the city.

"Citizen Lem, I am pleased that you could meet with me so promptly."

"I was happy to comply, citizen," Piet said. Despite the implicit threat of the shadowy figures in the background, he found feeling threatened by this personage difficult.

"I've heard so much about you. It's interesting to meet at last."

Like I was a video star, he thought.

She continued, "Hopefully you can assist me, well, us, with a pressing problem."

"Us?" He thought she looked excited and troubled about something.

She named the two or three people who ran the city, then, not waiting for his response, continued,

"We need your knowledge of the Subs to locate the headquarters of an important enemy of the Conclave. Sadly, we will have to terminate this traitor rather than sending him to the stasis chamber. The Conclave issued a special dispensation for this."

She gave him a minute to process this unusual information before she continued.

"Naturally, the Conclave regrets having to go to such extremes. Nor are we asking you to become personally involved in the termination. A group of special forces have that assignment."

"Who is this citizen? Have I heard of him?"

"The traitor is known as the Sojourner. He is the leader of a growing religionist movement that believes in the Man in the Sky."

"I'm not familiar with the group. We have few religionists in the Subs." Except me and the other Osirans, Piet thought.

"Oh, I know," she gushed. "But, well, this group is dangerous. At the very least, it is committed to forcing the Conclave to sanction its own version of religionism. It may have an ultimate goal of overthrowing the Conclave. Its influence is growing among all classes of citizens. They even have agents in some crèches." She made a disapproving sound.

"Children are easily led," Piet temporized. "Do you have any idea of the whereabouts of this Sojourner citiz . . . traitor?"

"We believe he is in the Subs." She identified a location in a sparsely populated area that, probably not coincidentally, was under the protestors' camp.

"Exactly what do you want me to do?"

"Find the traitor, contact me, and lead the group to his hideout. That's all. And be careful. This person and his followers are dangerous. I'll worry about you." She sounded like she would, too. She stood up, terminating the conversation, then started to say something.

"I know," Piet stood himself and they fist bumped. "You want it done right now."

"Time is of the essence. We don't want the Sojourner to get away again."

"There are strangely dressed soldiers watching my home," Piet said.

"Yes, dear," she glanced at one of the shadows. "They are the ones who will take out the Sojourner." She patted Piet on the arm and bustled out, the shadows following.

11

In Deep Cove, details about the explosion were meager, and the residents of the villa were more concerned with the disappearance of Ana and Teegan. Only Oren was upset about the explosion, consulting his comm continually to catch intermittent reports when they came through. He seemed especially concerned about the exact location of the blast and details about casualties. At the morning meal, he pumped Colt and Jordi for information about the protestors' encampment, urging them to speculate on the numbers killed and injured.

"Don't be ghoulish, Oren," Ilsa finally said, "especially at table where citizens are trying to eat."

Her comment shut him up but he toyed with his food, causing Linnet to look anxiously at him.

Upon hearing that Colt and Jordi planned to go to the clinic to try to locate the healer, Rick rolled his eyes in Oren's direction, and said, "Don't you have something else to do?" Colt had not had time to decide what he was going to do with Oren although he understood and shared Rick and Ilsa's concerns.

"I would like Oren to accompany us to the clinic in the aircar, if you don't mind," Colt said to Rick. The aircar had returned to the villa sometime during the night. The onboard navigation system was not informative, seemingly indicating that it had returned from the village.

"We could walk," Jordi said angrily. "It isn't far."

"I'd rather take the aircar. We might need to do some exploring," Colt said with finality, looking pointedly at both Jordi and Oren; the latter seemed on the verge of objecting.

Shortly thereafter, the three men headed for the nearby clinic.

"I could operate the controls on the aircar," Jordi whispered to Colt. "We don't need this clown."

Colt ignored him and watched the passing scenery, trying to catch sight of any overhead security satellites.

The little settlement looked much as it had the day the girls disappeared. The main feature was the two-story clinic, with its neat garden oriented around the statues of the elders. A few patients shambled along the paths. Across the street, a couple of big, powerful fusion bikes were propped up outside the bathhouse but no citizens were in sight.

"I hate this place," Jordi said.

"I would like to get back to the city myself," Colt said in a conciliatory tone. Since being seriously wounded by Irene Thorne's shotgun, Jordi's normally sunny, laid-back disposition had disappeared and he had become querulous and demanding.

"You and Oren take a walk over to the bathhouse and chat them up, ask them if they have heard anything about the girls. While you're there, try to find out who runs the two fusion bikes."

Oren was already eyeing the bikes and comparing them with the bike he had left hidden in the city. Colt was confident he could ask a million questions about the vehicles and Jordi could learn something about the riders.

Colt entered the clinic and requested a meeting with Healer Bruxton, only to be told that he had not returned from vacation. The bored receptionist had no idea when he would be coming back. She offered to contact the healer's assistant, a worried-looking young woman in wrinkled scrubs who appeared in due course. She brightened when she saw Colt. "You're a friend of Bartolo?" she said. "I saw you talking with him the other day. Is he coming back soon?"

"Not a friend exactly. I need to discuss treatment for my wife. He cared for her father, the citizen who was killed in the explosion at the clinic. She is still upset about it."

"I was working that day. It was very strange, that explosion. It blew a hole in the wall but no one could account for the source. Healer Bruxton was very puzzled, excited."

"Do you know where we can find him? It's important." He smiled, confidingly, he hoped.

"I wish I could find him, myself. He's our only healer sanctioned to do dental reconstruction and other major procedures. He's also our only healer sanctioned to deal with mental conditions. We're holding several cases for him." She looked irritated then glanced at the receptionist, who was engrossed in a video, and walked slowly toward the entrance, talking to Colt over her shoulder.

"He's been gone a lot lately. I'm afraid he'll leave permanently and then what will we do. There aren't enough healers as it is. I think he only works here because . . . ." She stopped suddenly and looked once more at the receptionist. "Anyway, he's gone a lot. He had just got back when you talked to him the other day."

"Back from the city, you mean?" Colt said.

She looked at him. "You some kind of investigator?" She looked indecisive, folded her arms. "I guess I don't care. I think he comes here because it gives him an excuse to explore the countryside around here for artifacts. Items from before the plague. I think he has a little business selling them."

"Ah," Colt said, "The authorities do not encourage that kind of thing. But I don't care. I'm just interested in finding the citizen."

"I don't know this for sure, of course," she waved a hand in front of her face to indicate the information had come from the air, the merest rumor, "but he might even be in the dead city."

Colt whistled. "Yeah? A dead city. Now that I did not know about. Where is it?"

"Up the coast a few klicks. I understand it was a big resort in the old days, very beautiful. There were homes all around here. Every time you dig a hole you find something old. But the city has all kind of objects in good condition. I'm told." She added and looked away.

"You think Healer Bruxton might be up there

looking for artifacts."

"It wouldn't surprise me," the assistant said. She swore as her comm bracelet made an angry noise. "That's all I know." She turned and walked back toward the clinic.

12

A dead city. Colt had always had a hankering to explore one of the vast abandoned cities that were left from the plague years. The Conclave forces had gone through each one, helping the remaining citizens to leave and resettle in safer locales. They destroyed all the dangerous items, books, especially, because they carried the deadly paper virus, but also films and other media that could harbor plague. Because no one could be sure they had completely eradicated all remaining germs, such items were forbidden to anyone not explicitly sanctioned by the authorities. Periodically the security satellites would spot citizens trying to return or searching for valuable items in the ruins and would send in troops to evict them.

If Healer Bruxton was sneaking into the dead city and retrieving artifacts to sell on the underground antiquities market, that would explain the expensive jewelry he had been wearing. Colt kicked himself for not realizing that the amber beads he affected were probably priceless.

Jordi and Oren were across the street looking at the two fusion bikes when Colt emerged from the clinic.

In the bright sunlight, Colt thought Jordi's skin showed up more pale than usual and he had become painfully thin. Engrossed in his own concerns, he had not noticed his friend's continuing physical deterioration. He probably wouldn't be doing him any favors by dragging him off to explore a dead city.

Oren continued poking around the bikes but Jordi saw Colt and crossed the street. He cocked his head toward the bikes. "Couple of bumpkins looking for funky sex. The proprietor of the bathhouse has a little sex club in the back. I think our little religionist disapproved."

Colt ignored Jordi's jibe.

"I want to do a little exploring here in town. The healer has a rental place and I plan to take a look at it."

"Looking for a rental of your own?" Jordi laughed.

"Something like that."

"What are you looking for?"

"A map, coordinates, directions, artifacts. The healer's assistant mentioned, strictly between us, that he collects artifacts from a dead city up the coast. Let's just say I'm curious about this citizen. He seems to have interests besides healing."

"Do you think this will lead to Ana and Teegan?"

"It might."

"Then lets gather up the bumpkin and check it out."

"You sure you're up to this, buddy? You look strung out." Colt rested a hand on his friend's bony shoulder.

"Anything for Teegan," Jordi said.

They left the aircar in front of the hospital, and having gathered Oren, walked into the little town. In the central square, they stopped at a little teashop and enquired for the location of Healer Bruxton's residence. A waiter eyed the three strangers inquisitively but shrugged and gave them directions.

The little cottage, a couple of rooms with a veranda in the rear, sat on the outmost edge of the town. An aircar charger was secured behind a locked grill at the back of the building. The veranda was not visible from other homes in the area, which appeared to be empty while their residents were at work.

Oren took at look at the charger and remarked that the aircar must be quite powerful. "That's an expensive charger for a small house like this." He remarked.

"This is a rental. He lives in the city, according to his assistant." As Colt talked, he wandered over to the double doors that opened off the veranda.

Reaching into his boot, he pulled out a large knife and inserted it between the doors, twisting. With a loud crack, the doors opened.

Other than that nothing happened. Colt had wondered if the healer had booby-trapped them in some way. He carefully opened the doors and entered the room, Oren and Jordi following.

"We shouldn't do this," Oren protested. "Its wrong to break into a citizen's house."

Still he followed them into the house and looked around. The little bungalow was barebones. A living room and kitchen combination, a small bedroom, and a water closet. The bedroom closet held a few items including healer's tunics.

They wandered around, opening drawers and checking out the refrigerator. They found the keys to the charging station but nothing else.

Colt swore. "He must have everything on his personal computer.

"At least with the key to the charging station, we can charge the aircar. Save Rick some cash."

"You don't want to do that," Oren said hastily. "If you do that, the other vehicle's programming will override the programming in Rick's vehicle."

Colt looked at him. "You mean, if we plug our aircar into his charging station, his programming will show up on our car's system?"

Oren looked at him like he was stupid. "Well, yes. That's how it works."

In almost no time, they had recovered their aircar from in front of the clinic and were looking at the display.

Two destinations of interest were programmed in: a location by the coast in the heart of what looked like a huge dead city and a spot a few klicks from their present location, apparently in open country.

A third, of less interest, was one of the entrances to the city, probably near his urban residence.

"I say we check out this spot in the countryside, see what's so interesting there that it would be programmed in the aircar." Colt stood back to let the two men precede him in the vehicle.

"I want to go back to Rick's and check on Linnet," Oren said. "I can walk. You guys go without me."

Colt merely pointed to the aircar and said, "We

might need you."

"We should swing by and let them know where we are going. The comm frequencies are still not working." Oren entered the aircar reluctantly.

Colt entered the aircar, blocking Oren's exit, and punched in the destination on the display.

"Why worry them needlessly," he said pleasantly.

The aircar rose silently to its cruising altitude and whooshed off into the desert.

13

The aircar skimmed through the open country, occasionally passing ruins of villas, old chimneys still standing, bridges to nowhere.

The land they were traversing was flat with mountains in the distance. Their path was not in sight of water but they could tell from the aircar's display that the shoreline was close by on their right.

Gradually the flat land began to be punctuated with larger ruins when multistory buildings had fallen in upon themselves but not yet returned to the earth. They saw no one. Colt and Jordi made sure their weapons were easily available. Oren claimed not to be armed.

When the display indicated that they were near their destination—a large pile of weatherbeaten rubble—Colt ordered Oren to set the aircar down. They would approach on foot.

Colt could tell that Oren wanted to refuse, but he and Jordi pushed him ahead. As they walked, Colt tried to decide whether Oren was afraid of the ruins, as many citizens were, or if he was afraid of something else. Colt knew many religionists had strange beliefs and fears about invisible beings and monsters and such. As he watched Oren's gait, he tried to gather information about the young man's state of mind. He had grown up in the countryside, maybe even hunted the dangerous wild animals that began roaming freely after the plague and needed to be destroyed. He had to be familiar with weapons, if not for hunting, for protecting the community's livestock from raiding parties. Linnet had told Colt of the community's small, but very valuable, herd of domesticated animals used for producing milk and cheese. Very occasionally, she had told a skeptical Colt, they were killed and eaten. The idea revolted Colt, but Linnet had explained that some very wealthy citizens had developed a taste for animal flesh and could obtain a special dispensation from the C.E. to consume it at special celebrations.

Oren moved gracefully across the uneven ground all the while looking around fearfully. As they approached the ruin, they had to climb over unstable piles of debris; Oren had no problem maintaining his footing, unlike Jordi, who was beginning to weaken.

When they finally came to the main wall of the ruin, they found a narrow opening. It was tall enough to walk through, but Colt thought, defensible. Oren, who they had been keeping in the lead, stopped before the doorway and refused to enter.

"Okay, Oren," Jordi said harshly. "Tell us what you are afraid of. Have you been here before? Are there fellow religionists hiding in the ruins?" He prodded Oren meaningfully with the conventional pistol he held.

Oren was practically in tears. He cowered away from the entrance.

"Demons, there are demons in the ruins." He grabbed at Jordi, who stepped back.

"Demons?" Colt queried. "Is this a religionist thing?"

Suddenly Oren looked wary. He started talking too fast. *He's not a very good liar*, Jordi thought.

"No, no, not religionist. Just facts. Everyone knows the ruins are forbidden because of germs and stuff left over from the old days. The paper virus is still in old books. Dangerous animals, cats, dogs; they are all infected. And demons are deadly."

Jordi looked interested. He started to say something, but Colt interrupted him, "We don't have time for this. We can talk about demons later. Let's go see what Healer Bruxton was hiding."

"All right," Oren straightened. "But they don't carry weapons. They don't need them. It can just look at you and you'll die."

Just before he stepped through the archway, he turned and said, "And they can walk through solid walls."

"You ever hear of a fusion grenade?" Jordi asked, following him.

"No," Oren answered.

Jordi turned and grinned at Colt. A fusion grenade could make an opening in a solid wall large enough for an adult citizen, or demon, to walk through.

The tunnel made a quick right and led to a space that had been cleared in front of what had probably once been an outbuilding. It was small and detached from the rest of the ruin; a new-looking door had been fitted neatly into a study looking frame. The door was open.

Before Colt could stop him, Oren walked through the entrance, then stopped.

"Oh, dear," he said.

Jordi, following him, screamed. Teegan Petrie was stretched out on the floor, obviously dead, a knotted scarf buried deep in her neck.

Jordi fell to his knees by her side, bereft. He took her hand, crying and repeating, "cold, cold."

Colt was shaken. He hurried into the next room, fearful of finding Ana also strangled, but the room was empty of everything except a makeshift camping kitchen. A privy had been knocked together behind the building.

Back in the main room, Jordi was sobbing and pulling at his hair in agitation.

"Demons," Oren whispered.

The chamber was clearly used as a storeroom for artifacts from the dead city. Shelves lined the walls; labels in old style writing identified various household items, some books, calendars using the old system of uneven months, fragile appearing fabrics. Clear boxes held jewelry and old timepieces that were avidly sought after by collectors.

"Wow, this stuff is worth a fortune." Colt reached for one of the boxes as Oren grabbed his arm. "Don't touch it, it's probably contaminated," the young citizen said.

"I thought you were afraid of demons." Colt shook his hand off, but he didn't pick up the box.

He checked the rest of the items in the room, a desk and chair, a daybed, bottles of water. He scrutinized the desk closely but found nothing of interest, no computer, no files.

"The demons were apparently interested enough to take the healer's computer, which would contain his records."

Jordi suddenly stood up and grabbed Colt's arm, "Why is she here? How did she get here?"

"She came here with the healer and Ana. He was supposed to be helping hide Ana from Chandler Besdine. Arlo sent a message from the city that Chandler wants Ana."

"So all that crap about the bathhouse was a trick?" Jordi face was unpleasantly red. "Why didn't you tell me?"

"Teegan thought you would worry."

Colt rubbed his own face. He felt dazed. The idea of Bartolo Bruxton killing Teegan was unbelievable. Teegan had been occupying herself having an affair with Bruxton while Linnet nursed Jordi. He knew something about Ana and Elvistine and he had said he was willing to help Ana, for a price.

"Was he another one of her men?" Jordi demanded.

Colt shrugged.

"It was demons," Oren said.

"Why would demons kill Teegan? And where are Ana and Bruxton?"

Colt could answer neither question, and Jordi looked terrible.

"We need to get back to Deep Cove," Colt said.

Jordi clutched at Colt's arm. "What about Teegan? We can't just leave her body here. She should be cremated."

"Or buried, like the old time people did." Oren piped up.

Jordi and Colt both shuddered.

"You can use your fusion pistol, disappear her," Jordi said. "We can just leave her body here for animals to find."

Colt refused to use his fusion pistol on Teegan. He was coming to realize that simply having people disappear raised more questions than were desirable. Besides the charge in his fusion pistol was low. They argued about the issue for some time; neither Colt nor Jordi liked the idea of burying her body in the earth. The idea was repugnant to them. Finally they decided to wrap her body in one of Healer Bruxton's ancient textiles and cover it with heavy stones. The dry air of the desert would preserve it until they could return at some future time with the necessary chemicals and cremate it.

They proceeded to carry out the plan despite Colt's impatience to return to Deep Cove. He wanted to get in touch with Arlo and Piet, to enlist their help in finding Ana.

As they piled the last rock on Teegan's corpse, Oren knelt by her body and bowed his head. Jordi had turned away toward the aircar, but, when he turned and saw Oren's kneeling posture, he ran toward him, intending to kick him in the head. Colt grabbed him and made a shushing gesture.

"I'll get that religionist bastard," Jordi said.

"Not right now," Colt insisted.

Unaware, Oren joined them and they returned to Rick and Ilsa's villa.

14

Only Linnet was happy to see Oren among those returning from the visit to the clinic, but she, Rick, and Ilsa became concerned when the trio exited the aircar. Their attitudes signaled that something dreadful had happened. When Colt explained, everyone was deeply concerned about finding Teegan's body. Rick and Ilsa were already scared out of their wits at the presence of Oren and the threat he posed. Teegan's murder, however remote in distance, seemed to offer yet another challenge to their peace of mind. Jordi dwelt on Oren's religionist concerns about demons, further alarming Ilsa.

Linnet did not share their concerns; she thought Rick and Ilsa were overreacting. Once again she took charge of Jordi, who was in a pitiable state, hustling him into his bedroom and going to prepare tea heavily laced with an herbal soporific.

Colt was anxious to contact Piet and Arlo. Comm frequencies were still not reliable in the vicinity of the city. Little news was forthcoming; videos kept repeating the original message.

Colt decided he would try to get into the city. Once there he could easily reach the Subs. The aircar would stop outside the perimeter, and Colt would move across country, scoping out a way to bypass the guards.

Oren begged to go with him, to recover his bike, and Colt briefly considered the option. If Oren went with him, then took off, they would be done with him and the threat he posed. Colt wasn't sure he liked the idea of Oren wandering around on his own while Linnet, whom he seemed genuinely to care for, stayed in Deep Cove.

Colt decided to keep him where the others could keep an eye on him.

"I don't trust religionists," he told Rick. "You and Jordi keep an eye on him. If he starts to run, use your judgment. I know Jordi is armed. Do you have a weapon?" Rick nodded.

"I would just let him go, but use your judgment."

"He could bring the authorities down on us," Rich said. Colt merely nodded. He couldn't tell them to kill Oren. He himself had killed lots of citizens while in the military, but it was a decision everyone had to make for himself.

Rick's aircar dropped Colt outside the ring of new sentry posts that had been set up around the city to maintain the lockdown.

The new posts augmented already existing posts operated by the municipal authorities. As he jogged, the light dimmed as the pall that always hovered over the city displaced the bright daylight of the countryside. He mulled over his options. He carried an expired pass that he had previously used to go to Deep Cove and considered using it to talk his way back into the city. The idea spooked him. What if the authorities were looking for him?

The aircar had used the healer's coordinates and dropped him near a residential section of the city. If he swung south he would find himself in the area where huge conventionally powered lorries brought products into the city from outlying farms and distant ports. Linnet had originally snuck into the city from her community by hiding in such a vehicle.

The manufacturing district offered another busy point of access. But Colt knew nothing about either area and finally opted for the more appealing option of pure stealth. The light was growing steadily darker, and Colt had confidence in his skills. Eventually he easily entered the city. The guards at the temporary security posts were intently watching videos that sounded like news releases. As he slipped by unnoticed, he watched for security satellites and was puzzled when he saw none.

Back on the dark streets, he felt at home, happier than he had been in the countryside, in Deep Cove. He had emerged through an alley near his neighborhood, not too far from Sandy's, a café where he was well-known and good friends with the bartender. His original intention had been to directly enter the Subs and find Piet Lem but the proximity of the café changed his mind. He could use a drink and the bartender would know what was going on. He couldn't stay on the streets, which were teeming with militia and local authorities. He even saw some regular C.E. military in the distance. A few furtive-looking citizens hurried on urgent errands, avoiding eye contact.

The door to Sandy's was unlocked, the long narrow bar empty. At the rear, the bartender rested his hand on an ancient but deadly shotgun until he recognized Colt. Then he brightened and rushed forward.

"Colt, man. It's good to see you. I heard you went to the country."

He led him to the rear of the café, pouring them both neat shots of bourbon

They toasted the elders. "What the fuck is going on?" Colt asked, feeling revivified by the alcohol.

"Don't know, my friend. Explosions in the protestors' encampment, strange armed soldiers in the Subs."

Colt was aghast. "What kind of soldiers? Has there been fighting in the Subs?"

"Not that I know of. Just heard reports about large groups of armed strangers."

"What about Piet Lem and Beau?"

"No one knows. He and his people haven't been seen, but they wouldn't be, if they didn't want to. The strangers are in uniform, but no one recognizes their insignia or knows what service they were in."

He topped off their drinks.

Colt settled onto a bar stool while the bartender filled him in on the few sparse details. The local authorities were not giving out much news; the city was still on lockdown except for essential business.

"They don't seem to be bothering normal citizens," he added. "They are very jumpy, though, and discipline is lax. Several soldiers have ducked in here for a quick one, which is unsanctioned behavior for them. Unfortunately they don't seem to know anything. The officers just keep telling them to keep their eyes open." He laughed then leaned forward, confidentially, even though the bar was completely empty. "I understand there are some big games coming down now that everyone is forced off the streets and out of the clubs."

Colt brightened up; he felt energy pouring through him, anticipation.

"Yeah, big games. Where at?"

The bartender mentioned a name. Colt knew the place. He knew all the clandestine Mah Jongg parlors. This one was frequented by wealthy players. Colt happened to have quite a bit of old money stashed nearby in his flat.

He borrowed the bartender's comm and called the number he had for Arlo, who answered immediately. Their conversation was brief. Arlo was at the flat and would stay there if Colt came immediately. The comm frequencies were chancy, Arlo said, so don't bother to call again.

The palms of Colt's hands itched and he felt sweat beginning to prickle at his underarms. A quick trip to his flat and he would be flush with old money. The other players would be tired from hours of play. He, himself, was fresh, invigorated.

He downed the rest of the drink and left the bar.

Colt drifted through the quiet streets, meeting few people, none in uniform. The night was advanced, and most people would be asleep. The huge buildings were silent and dark. The stairwell in his building was dimly lit and, as he hurried toward his flat, his mind was full of money, luck, and the constellations of tiles, perfect winning hands.

Colt found Arlo dressed for the street with his backpack packed. Arlo asked about Ana and Teegan. He had once been in love with Ana. Colt told him there had been some problems and asked about the explosions in the protestors' camp. Arlo told him what he knew. Arlo had heard nothing about strange military in the Subs that the bartender at Sandy's had mentioned.

They dithered for a while, trying to decide whether to stay in the flat or go to the Subs to see for themselves what was going on. Colt had a lot to tell Arlo about Ana and about Teegan's murder, but he felt unsafe in the flat. Sadly, it no longer spoke security and refuge to him. He thought Arlo would be devastated by Teegan's death since, based on her comments about Arlo before the Irene incident, he and Teegan had apparently had some kind of relationship. Colt didn't want to drop the news on him until they reached a place where he could process the information. Neither Arlo's nor Colt's comms were working. Finally, rather than walking into a situation in the Subs, they decided to go to the House of Blue Leaves. Sparrow usually had good information.

15

The House was locked up tight but knocking loudly on the door brought a young citizen, dressed in street clothes, looking wary, to open the door for them. They followed him upstairs where everything was strangely quiet. The blue lights that gave the house its name were off and the resulting ambience was sad and dusty. One light was on in the cafe and Arlo and Colt were surprised to see Piet and Beau at a table with Sparrow.

The young citizen brought in a tray from the kitchen with tea for the newcomers, then faded away. The mood at the table was somber.

"Welcome to the House of Blue Leaves," Sparrow finally opened the conversation. "I'm afraid the lockdown has affected the quality of our services."

"We heard there were strange soldiers in the Subs," Arlo got right to the point. "That's why we came to Sparrow's rather than going there. We didn't expect to find you and Beau."

Colt spoke before Piet could explain. "Before you

bring us up to date, I have bad news, shocking news." He looked at Arlo and put his hand on the other man's forearm. "Teegan Petrie is dead. She was murdered helping Ana to hide. And Ana is gone, presumably kidnapped."

They all looked at him, stunned. Arlo put his head in his hands. "What happened?" His voice was harsh.

Colt recounted the events beginning with the call from Arlo about Chandler Besdine, the plot to hide Ana in the healer's cottage, locating the healer's aircar, and finding Teegan strangled in the artifact storage. Halfway through the tale, Sparrow called for a bottle of cognac.

Colt's audience was enthralled.

Piet and Beau were barely acquainted with Teegan but Arlo was in shock. "Why kill Teegan?" he asked.

Colt looked squarely at Arlo. "You have any ideas? Immediately before the incident in Deep Cove, Teegan told me she was going to leave Jordi and run away with you. She said she wanted to help you with your mission. She said you were in love with her."

Arlo sighed and rubbed his eyes with his sleeve. "Colt, you know Teegan. She was a fantast, a seeker. She got caught up in things, new things. I think Jordi bored her; his love and acceptance bored her. She wanted excitement. She and I often talked about ways to bring down the Conclave. In the old days we spent a lot of time together. She didn't really know anything about my. . .er. . .mission."

"Did you sleep with her?" Sparrow asked conversationally.

Arlo gave him a dirty look. "No."

Then he sighed again, "I kind of regret that now. She was so beautiful."

"So why did the healer kill her? If it was the healer," Piet asked.

"I think she was in the way. For some reason, the healer just wanted Ana. I wasn't going to mention this to spare Arlo's feelings, but she was getting it on with the healer."

"And you think the healer took Ana to the dead city?" Beau asked.

Colt shrugged. "It's just a feeling," he said. "Based on the programming in his aircar, he is familiar with the dead city. I could make a better determination if I knew what he wanted with her. Yonatan Belasco may have some information about him as a fellow healer."

They explained that Yonatan was still helping with the injured in the protestors' camp.

"This is troubling." Piet said. "If he was a simple pervert and wanted a woman for some unsanctioned sexual activity, he would have taken Teegan. They were already lovers. She was more beautiful than Ana and probably more uninhibited."

"No offense, Colt," he added.

"None taken, Citizen Lem. You're right. Is there a bounty on Ana?"

"Not that I've heard of." That settled that question. If there was a bounty on anyone, Piet and Grupo Uno heard about it.

"Do you think Chandler had anything to do with Ana's disappearance? He is anxious to find her," Piet said.

"What contact would the healer have with Chandler?" Colt asked, looking at the others around the table.

Piet said, "Who else could he be working for? Tillman?"

"Tillman's in the stasis chamber," Arlo said.

"I doubt that," Piet said, "I think he never was in a stasis chamber. I think he is around somewhere. But he is not our problem, at least not at the moment. I doubt either he or Chandler have anything to do with the healer. I will go willingly to the dead city with you, citizen Bede, to search for Ana, but first I have pressing business in the city." He told them about his meeting with the high authority, his unwanted mandate to find the citizen known as the Sojourner so the strange soldiers could terminate him.

Arlo was keenly interested. "Are you going to do it? Grupo Uno never had a policy of interfering with religionists in the Subs." Arlo claimed to be an Osiran, as were Piet and Beau.

Piet shrugged. "I will try to communicate with the citizen before I turn him over to the soldiers." Beau looked surprised. This was news to him.

Piet stood up. "Let's get some sleep," he said. "We need to make plans, but not tonight."

Sparrow operated part of his business as a regular hotel, albeit not open to the general public. With the help of the waiter, his guests were shown to rooms and made comfortable. Sparrow and the young waiter finally withdrew to Sparrow's private apartment.

16

Once everyone was settled, Colt took from his backpack the stash of old money he had recovered from its hiding place in the flat. The big games would be continuing.

He drifted downstairs in his silent way and into a ghostly night city.

The streets of the entertainment district, usually then at their most raucous, were empty. As a result of the lockdown, the 24/7 clubs were dark, the small all-night cafes shuttered. The streetlights themselves seemed dimmer than usual.

His path was downward. Gambling parlors were always underground, in rooms behind back rooms, in basements of abandoned buildings. Many, but not all, were naturally in the Subs, but wealthy upside entrepreneurs avoided the Subs. The upside games tended to be more expensive. Colt was flush with old money; he would stay upside.

He found himself breathing more deeply, walking faster, anticipating the surf of adrenalin that inevitably accompanied his forays into what he considered his real life, his authentic being. The vague shadow of desperate need usually provided an edge.

Instead he felt empty, indifferent. He unsuccessfully willed himself to think of nothing but the coming hands, the tiles, the noise as they crashed onto the tables. He reminded himself that he especially relished watching the practiced inscrutable faces, looking for small nervous twitches, identifying unnecessary gestures that betrayed players' emotions.

By the time he arrived at the site, the focused exhilaration he usually reveled in had not come.

The room was large, loud, low ceilinged, brightly lit, just perfect. He was known to the doorkeeper; and they exchanged friendly fist bumps. The major domo knew him, as well. Several players recognized him and dropped miniscule acknowledgements.

A seat was not immediately available so he wandered over to the bar that sold all the liquors and drugs players needed to enhance their game. They had Colt's drug of choice, and he briefly thought about purchasing it. Maybe it would help him get his edge back. Instead, he asked for a glass of tea and strolled around watching the action, feeling cold and alienated.

A seat opened up and all eyes went to the major domo, who nodded to Colt. He strolled over the table, he sat and nodded to the other three gamesters; it was as if nothing was different.

Sparrow was trying to get some sleep. He had even sent the young waiter back to his quarters. Earlier in the day, a few customers had snuck in, despite the lockdown, bringing all kinds of frightening rumors, scaring the kids.

The older workers were concerned, too, but for different reasons. They remembered stories of the chaos, death, and violence, cities destroyed, homes and farms burned, before the Conclave of Elders brought order to the planet. The kids thought they might be killed; the others thought they might lose their way of life.

Sparrow lay awake wondering why the Conclave's military had not arrived in force to settle the situation.

Early the next morning, Yonatan staggered home, exhausted and covered in blood and dirt. He managed to get into the sonic shower, then poured some tea and cognac down his throat. When he finally got to bed, he immediately passed out.

A few hours later, he awakened, somewhat rested but still frightened, no, he thought, terrified, by the stories the wounded protestors had told him.

He didn't feel much better when Sparrow called and invited him to breakfast at the House of Blue Leaves. Sparrow said Piet Lem wanted to see him.

He felt even worse when he was leaving his flat and the concierge handed him an unmarked package. Inside was a priceless pre-plague ebony box, hinged as if to reveal fine jewelry. Nestled in the silk lining were six of the deadly cockroaches, their blue eyes blinking, each embossed with a different icon. They were centered around a remote activator with six buttons, each embossed with an icon matching one of the receivers. The silver healers' sigil was embossed on the back of each unit. Tucked inside the cover was a directive from the Conclave of Elders. As usual, it was a platinum plate engraved in the C.E.'s combination of old writing and icons. It directed him by name to use the enclosed modality in those cases where a complete cure of unsanctioned religionist beliefs could not be effected. It ended by completely absolving him of any harm that might come to the patients under such treatment. Nowhere did it imply that he should use his judgment.

He put the box in his briefcase and headed out for breakfast at Sparrow's, starting what he just knew would be another terrible day.

17

Piet and Beau were up early the next morning. Beau joined Sparrow's young chef in the cafe kitchen, putting together a pot of soup and soft rice. Piet drank tea and tried to raise various citizens on his comm. Finally he told Beau, "Go roust Colt and Arlo. They've had enough sleep. We need to decide what to do when we return to the Subs."

Before Beau could leave the cafe, Yonatan entered carrying his black healer's bag. He looked terrible, wan and unkempt. Beau placed a bowl of soup in front of him and he ignored the spoon, picked it up and drank ravenously. Apologizing for his uncouth manners, he gulped down a glass of tea.

When he finished eating he sat staring blankly into space, contemplating something horrible, his hands flat on the table.

Beau was especially shaken to see this self-possessed and accomplished adult so distraught. He started to speak, to prod the older man, but his father caught his attention, made a little gesture. Behind them, Arlo slipped into the room, and catching the mood of the room, remained silent.

They watched as the healer rallied, tightening his hands on the table, rubbing his lips together. Finally, he look at them, smiling, some of his old composure regained.

He went to a sideboard and poured a stiff slug of cognac in his tea. When he regained his seat and smiled again, Beau felt a sense of dread, a sense that he going to hear something else that would change his world.

"I apologize, my friends and colleagues. Talking with the surviving protestors, I find that we in the city have been out of touch, insulated. Chaos is coming from beyond our walls; sliding over the surrounding countryside, even soon, I'm afraid, into the heart of the Subs. As the protestors were dying last night from the explosions, many were from far away where they had fled from devastation, war, and worse." He took a large swig of tea. "They told us the danger is coming from the sky."

"Another plague?" Beau whispered.

"No plague. Just simple death."

They were all silent, except Arlo, who noisily finished off his tea.

"I was afraid of this," Arlo said.

"Afraid of what, my friend, death, devastation, chaos?" Piet waved his glass ironically.

"Airships," Arlo said.

"Airships," Beau repeated. "You mean big helicopters?"

"No, helicopters are strictly owned and used by the Conclave. They cannot efficiently carry a lot of cargo and they are noisy. Airships are completely different.

"Irene Thorne had a helicopter," Beau interrupted.

"Yeah, she did, didn't she?" Arlo smiled grimly then continued.

He continued, "While I was away I spent a couple of years at a commune in the foothills that made a living distilling liquor. For years they would sneak into dead cities and find cases, even warehouses full of booze, rebottle it, and sell it. It doesn't spoil, you know. When they had pillaged all they could, they found a guy who could teach them how to distill different kinds of liquor. It's pretty good. They developed a good business." He nodded at the bottle of bourbon. "They probably made that."

"And, airships? Do they run on liquor?" Beau said impatiently.

"No, airships are just big gas bags. The master distiller at the commune was a graduate of one of the Conclave's private technical universities. They have a number of training and research facilities focusing on developing technologies. Many are desperately trying to find ways to address the declining population, but they have other agendas as well. An effort was underway to modify the fusion energy used in aircars to achieve higher altitudes. Aircars are pretty limited in how high they can go. It has something to do with the planet's magnetic center. But one of their tame scientists was looking through some old technical books and came up with the bright idea of developing a gas that was light enough to float a vehicle several thousand meters in the air."

"How large a vehicle?" Yonatan asked.

"A pretty good sized vehicle, I think. The master

distiller told me this story after he made a trip back to the lab for an Elders' Day celebration or some event. A buddy of his was working on the project."

"The protestors said there were dragons in the air." Yonatan said. "Breathing fire."

"I'll bet they only appeared at night," Arlo said. "Creating lighted images of dragons would be easy."

"And they are dropping bombs," Beau said.

"Bombs and poison gas. If you can create a gas that will float an airship, you could create a gas that will kill people wholesale."

"Where were the strangers from?" Beau asked. "Could the strangers killed in the explosions in the Subs be aliens from another universe?" Beau looked to Yonatan as the most educated citizen among them.

"Aliens?" Arlo and Yonatan were taken aback at the question, as Piet sighed and said, "Beau was quite taken with the idea of a portal between universes such as that opened by Colt's wife and Dr. Elvistine. He is convinced aliens could come through it."

"Most of the strangers in the protestors' camp looked like people from far away. Some were from the land of volcanoes. But they could be aliens," the healer responded angrily, "If they looked like you and me and registered the same on diagnostic tools, I wouldn't know whether or not they were aliens. The strangers last night claimed to be from distant parts of the planet. Some were fluent in their own unsanctioned tongues but not so much in the sanctioned tongue, so I was limited in what I could learn. Some said they were mercenaries, hired to come to the city to establish a clandestine base in the Subs and wipe out the protestors, but they got caught in their own bombing raid."

"Besides," Yonatan continued thoughtfully, "how do you know what aliens from another dimension would look like. They might look like people from this planet but in their dimension they would look like something else entirely. Some deep scientists think we look like we do on this planet because of the environment. The elements that make up our bodies are the same elements that existed on the planet before we developed in our current form. In another dimension, they would develop based on the elements that existed in their home."

"Giant blobs," Beau said excitedly, "or giant grasshoppers, with armor."

"Why giant anything?" Yonatan asked, "Why not tiny blobs?"

"Then they wouldn't have brains," Beau protested.

"They might not have brains like we have, but they still might be able to conceptualize."

Beau looked puzzled.

"Think," Yonatan amended.

Seeing that Beau could continue this meaningless discussion for a long time, Piet interjected, "Did the strange soldiers in the protestors' camp know who hired them?" Piet asked.

"Who else, the C.E. hired them or so they believed. Their commander was one of the first killed in the attack so I did not talk with her."

18

Colt was bummed. He had done well most of the night, winning respectably, but his heart was not in it. The enchantment had fallen away. When the majordomo placed a novice at the table, Colt and the other experienced players were thrown off their game by the new player's dawdling and indecision. As soon as they could, they left the table. Colt was angry and relieved. He hurried outside, anxious to get back to Sparrow's place. As he walked quickly away, he almost failed to notice that he was being followed.

The usually intensely bright streetlights had been dimmed, presumably because of the lockdown, as a signal to townspeople to stay off the streets. The follower was decent—Colt could not actually see the citizen—but he had noticed a shadow that was moving slightly. The shadow betrayed itself by mimicking Colt's stops and starts. When he stopped to make sure he had securely stashed his remaining cash, the shadow stopped also. An expert would have kept moving, but slowly. The shadow's job was harder because the streets were mostly empty. A few early morning laborers and kiosk keepers were scuttling to work, disregarding the lockdown, but the city still lay in silence.

Having planned to simply return to his room and get some sleep, Colt was annoyed by the added problem. His first instinct was to lose the citizen and go home. Then he reconsidered. Perhaps this was a simple mugger, but his life had been so crazy lately, so many unknown citizens seemed interested in him, that he thought he would find out whether the citizen wanted to rob him, kill him, or something else.

Melting into the shadows, Colt vaulted easily onto the roof of a convenient kiosk, hunkering down, waiting for the follower to materialize.

He made sure both his weapons were handy.

A few minutes later a shadow detached itself from a wall and a citizen he did not recognize emerged into the filtered light of the street, presumably having abandoned the chase. Dropping from the roof to the sidewalk, Colt stood motionless, letting distance develop between them. Suddenly the other party spun around, a powerful weapon pointed in Colt's direction. Instinctively, Colt flung his knife, aiming for the front of the shoulder, to incapacitate the man's arm and force him to drop his heavy pistol. As he threw, the other man flinched, just enough that Colt's knife penetrated the front of his throat instead, severing his brain stem and killing him instantly. The pistol fell to the ground but mercifully did not discharge.

Chagrined, Colt quickly ran forward and dragged the body into a nearby doorway. Fortunately, the few bloodstains were invisible in the dim light. After removing his knife and wiping it clean on the man's uniform tunic, Colt took stock. His night vision was pretty good and even in the dim light he could see the man was from a distant part of the planet. He was wearing a distinctive patch of turquoise and coral beads, which Colt removed and stuck, in his pocket for future reference. He thought Piet might recognize it. He pushed up the dead man's sleeve to take the comm that presumably linked him to his unit to drop in a distant dumpster. Just above the comm, wrapped around the man's wrist was a string of worry beads similar to those owned by the missing healer.

Troubled, Colt took the worry beads and maintaining all the considerable stealth he was capable of, returned to the House of Blue Leaves.

"About time you got here," Arlo snarled, when Colt slouched into the cafe, suddenly exhausted. The smell of food was intoxicating and he hurried to the sideboard to help himself. He noted that Yonatan had arrived from his mission of mercy.

As Yonatan continued describing some of the strangers who had died in the explosion, Colt removed the fabric patch from his pocket and threw it on the table.

Yonatan looked at the patch on the table then at Colt. No one recognized it.

"Where did that come from? He asked.

"Someone was following me." Colt said.

"From the game?" Arlo sounded surprised.

"Nope, he had to have followed me to the game and waited for me to come out. Only certain people knew where that game was being held, and he was not one of them."

"Why are they following you?" Beau asked.

"Because they think I'll lead them to Ana, I guess."

"You didn't question him?" Beau asked.

"The citizen is dead. When he lost me, he thought I might be waiting to follow him, so he set a trap, pretended to give up, and when I showed myself, he tried to kill me."

"You should have disarmed him without killing him," Arlo said. Colt and Piet exchanged ironic glances since both knew Arlo could not disarm a chair.

"I intended to disarm him, but, unfortunately, he ducked as I threw my knife and instead of the shoulder, he took it in the throat."

"Too bad," Piet shook his head. "But you took his patch. Good thinking."

Colt held up the worry beads. "And I got this."

"It's not like you to steal from the dead, Colt." Piet said sadly. "Although they seem quite valuable."

"Yes, quite valuable. And unusual. And unsanctioned. Just like those worn by Healer Bruxton."

At the healer's name, Yonatan started. "Healer Bruxton, Bartolo Bruxton?" he said. "You're sure that was his name." At Colt's assent, Yonatan groaned. "He's supposed to be in a re-education camp. He's crazy. He's some kind of religionist. He was well connected, and I tried to cure him, but finally I had to send him away."

"Would he kill someone? Was he violent? I thought religionists were pacifistic," Colt asked, alarmed.

"There are all kinds of religionists," Yonatan said.

"Some are pacifistic but some feel justified by their beliefs to be violent, either to protect themselves or to get rid of other religionists. So, yes, fanatical religionists like Bruxton are comfortable with violence. He would undoubtedly kill someone if he thought it was congruent with his beliefs."

"But he was having an affair with Teegan. Is that okay for religionists, too?"

Yonatan laughed. "Anything's okay for religionists. Maybe he thought it was a way to convert her."

They all had a laugh at the idea of Teegan being converted. Even as he laughed, Colt found himself tremendously sad remembering their years of friendship, their good times together. And how much Jordi loved her.

He shook it off.

"My immediate concern is finding Ana and keeping her away from everybody; Chandler, the Conclave, the authorities, everybody." Colt said.

"How will you find her; you don't know where she is?" Beau asked, reasonably.

"I'm going to the dead city," Colt said. "Bruxton was familiar with it, and I'm betting he took Ana there. I was hoping you would help me."

Arlo immediately agreed to accompany Colt to the dead city. Moreover, he would try to establish communications with the whiskey commune where he had lived and worked for a few years. Someone there might have useful information about the dead city.

19

Piet was deeply troubled by the incursion into the Subs of the strange soldiers. He was anxious to determine how numerous they were and how extensively they had spread through the great underground world. Groupo Uno was not the only organized group in the Subs but it was the largest. Through the organization, Piet directed most of the lucrative trade in unsanctioned goods and services and his policy, like that of his uncle from whom he had inherited leadership, was to ignore any activity no matter how unsanctioned and illegal as long as it didn't directly threaten anyone under his cloak. There were areas of the Subs that he rarely visited, areas that were uninhabited, and some locations that were uninhabitable because dangerously unstable from earthquakes and construction activities. One such uninhabitable area was the area under the protestors' encampment.

In the aftermath of the plague, the area now taken over by the protestors had been the site of huge fusion furnaces that were used to do away with the tens of thousands of bodies of plague victims. The authorities had constructed a large building on the site with docks for unloading the body-bearing trucks and conveyor belts for carrying the bodies into the fusion furnace. Construction of the heavy building had undermined the area underground to an extent that it was unsafe to live there. Rock falls were common. Some citizens described toxic seepage from the ground above.

Once the building was no longer needed, it was gutted of useful equipment and left to slowly deteriorate. Because of its ghoulish history and rumored toxicity, residents of the city tended to give the area a wide berth until the protestors arrived. They finished razing the structure and used the rubble to build foundations for their tent city.

Still there were citizens of the Subs who knew that area and would be familiar with outsiders taking up residence, as was apparently the case with the Sojourner.

Piet would go to them. His plan, such as it was, would involve locating the area where the interlopers were staying, reconnoitering using the services of the Subs dwellers, then deciding the best way to contact the citizen known as the Sojourner. Only then would he alert the soldiers occupying his home.

And then, if all went as planned, he would accompany Colt to the dead city to, possibly, rescue Ana and avenge Teegan.

Ever since the betrayal by Rowan, Piet had felt reluctant to advertise his activities, even to his close associates in Grupo Uno. He accepted Colt's offer to accompany him and Beau in their attempt to contact the Sojourner. Colt was always an asset in a fight, and not a citizen to go off half-cocked.

Arlo and one of Piet's young lieutenants were off to locate his contact at the whiskey commune and gather intel on the dead city. The kid could get Arlo safely through the checkpoints and into an aircar for the trip.

Colt had never been as fascinated by the Subs as had Arlo and some of his other friends. He had occasionally visited Piet through the years and attended some of the underground clubs that sprung up from time to time. Once, when he was still cage fighting, he had participated in a brutal unsanctioned competition downside. Which he had won and promised himself never to do again.

He followed Piet and Beau through sections of the Subs where strange daylight seemed to emanate from the rock walls and everything seemed completely alien. Piet and Beau were sure of their location but Colt's excellent sense of direction deserted him immediately. He knew they must be heading toward the protestors' encampment and the path felt like it was sloping downward. He could hear water somewhere nearby. When he asked Piet about the sounds, he was told it was the river. Shortly thereafter they came upon a shallow stream that flowed away from them. Paths were worn away on both sides. Colt was beginning to believe no one really lived there when a pale personage of great antiquity and no teeth emerged from an opening on the other side of the water. He wore an unbelievably filthy robe of some sort. Piet jumped across to the other bank, fist bumped, then chatted briefly with the oldster. Old money changed hands. They fist bumped again and Piet jumped back, taking the lead, but saying nothing.

They followed the underground river for a while, encountering several more gruesome citizens, fist bumping and handing out old money. Finally, they left the river. As the path went uphill slightly, the air seemed lighter and cleaner. Piet turned and put a finger to his lips for silence and ducked into a little cave that had been cut into the wall.

One of Piet's contacts had reported seeing a personage wearing a robe and hood, whom Piet assumed was the Sojourner. Approximately a dozen of the personage's followers were using some storerooms built into the subbasement of a manufacturing plant that had once operated in the city. The building had been abandoned, although a few citizens squatted on the upper floors. The people they sought were in rooms just under the edge of the protestors' camp. A stairwell provided easy access to the city.

Beau and Colt followed Piet into the cave where they waited. They could see a wide corridor that led to the storerooms. A citizen of the Subs who was well acquainted with the area had gone ahead to report whether the coast was clear. They waited in silence for some time until another pale, unwashed specimen with the ubiquitous rotten teeth, sidled into the space. He and Piet fist bumped and the citizen whispered in Piet's ear then slipped out again.

Piet followed, stepping from the cave into the corridor, motioning for Colt and Beau to follow and again making a sign for silence. Colt checked his weapons, covering the rear.

The unwashed one preceded them as the corridor widened into a good sized space then waved and vanished into a dark tunnel that branched off to the left. The corridor continued forward past the entrances to the tunnel on the left and another on the right. As they passed the right-hand opening, citizens ran into the space, armed mostly with knives. They were not experienced fighters. Colt immediately disarmed two of them, dropping them to the floor. Piet used his own knife on another as a hooded figure appeared in the opening ahead. The figure paused, holding a knife of its own, then, taking careful aim, threw it hard, striking Beau in the groin. The hooded figure turned and fled. The one remaining fighter paused just long enough for Piet to strike him down before turning to Beau, who was bleeding profusely.

While Piet knelt by his son, pressing his jacket against the wound, Colt ran after the fleeing assailant. He passed through two storerooms and ran up a stairs that exited through the abandoned factory into a quiet city street. The street was empty. The buildings were mostly unoccupied; there would be many spots that would provide cover. There would also be squatters living in the shadows. Colt thought he might return at night and have a look around, chat up some of the locals. He was pretty confident they knew what was going on in the area.

In the meantime, he returned to the tunnel, where Piet was still kneeling by Beau, who was unconscious and very pale.

"I've called Yonatan," Piet said stoically. "At least the comms seem to be working again. I'm afraid we'll have to take Beau to a sanctioned clinic. He's very badly wounded."

Colt knelt beside the boy, taking his hand. It was unpleasantly cool and clammy. Piet meanwhile had grabbed one of the attackers who remained alive, although badly injured. Piet had a knife at his throat.

"Why did you attack us?" Piet showed the citizen the knife, then gently stuck the point into his throat.

"We had to protect the Sojourner," the citizen whispered. "Above everything."

"You're going to die," Piet said, nudging him with the point of his knife until an unpleasant little line of blood began to trickle down.

He held up the knife again. "See, that is your blood," he said.

"I know," the man looked upward, toward the ceiling, "I'm going to transition to the garden," he said.

"You'll transition to the garden in agony, citizen, unless you tell me where I can find this Sojourner. He tried to kill my son, and I will deal with him."

The citizen began to weep. "I'm going," he whispered. Then he uttered a name that meant nothing to either Piet or Colt and died.

Piet dropped the dead body to the floor and looked over at Colt, who was still holding Beau's hand. "He's hanging on," Colt said.

Between them they carried him up the stairs, so Yonatan would have no trouble following the signal on Piet's comm, then waited impatiently for him to arrive. When he finally reached them, he had medics with him and they took charge immediately. Yonatan merely shook his head when he saw the wound and hurried his assistants with their stretcher to the specially outfitted aircar.

When they had taken Beau away, Yonatan put his hand on Piet's arm. "He's very badly hurt. I've sent him to a special clinic I use for my private clients. They will provide the very best care."

"The authorities . . . ," Piet started to say.

"I'll take care of the authorities."

When Piet started to tell him what happened, Yonatan stopped him. "I've got to go," he said. "I'll be in touch immediately when I know anything." And left. Leaving Colt and Piet to stare at each other in angry silence, and fear.

They searched the bodies and found nothing useful. None were local citizens and nothing indicated where they were going. A search of the two storerooms revealed nothing they could use either. Several citizens had been living there and had recently packed up and left, not in a hurry. They did find a motion sensor, almost invisible, in the tunnel where they had been attacked.

They left the bodies where they were, knowing that the ghostly citizens of the Subs would quickly strip them of clothes and valuables and they would disappear into some stony recess far from the light of day.

As they returned through the tunnels, Colt's mood was oppressive. He was coming to dislike the unnatural warmth and ambient light seeping from above through invisible cracks. Knowing they were tracked by pale, hungry wraiths, potentially hostile— he was not convinced the motion detector alone had betrayed them—was unsettling. He found himself regretting the deaths of the patently inept citizens who had attacked them. They were religionists, unsanctioned and, admittedly, misguided, but not fighters, not soldiers. Colt had killed enemy soldiers in his years with the military and even, inadvertently, in his cage fighting days when opponents had died from their injuries. It was not wholly unusual. Any surviving sanctioned partners received nice bonuses. The unknown who had attacked him outside the gambling parlor was a soldier, and Colt had been defending himself.

Colt replayed the encounter in his mind. The four or five knife-wielding citizens, Colt had already forgotten the number, were clowns. The hooded one, their leader, had been skilled. He had aimed at Beau's groin, thrown the dagger firmly, precisely, at a spot that would not necessarily be immediately lethal, a wound to cause suffering. By attacking Beau he had doubled the suffering because, Colt concluded, the hooded one knew them, knew Piet Lem, knew Beau was his son.

"He knew you," Colt said.

"Yes," Piet did not look over his shoulder or pause in his grim tramping back to his end of the Subs. "And I knew him."

When Piet mentioned the hooded one's name, Colt was shocked.

"That makes no sense," he blurted.

Piet said nothing, shaking his head grimly and lengthening his strides.

20

At the clinic, Yonatan and his assistants had stabilized Beau; stopped the bleeding from his wound. Now they were carefully watching his reactions to the synthetic blood that flowed into him. Yonatan sat by his bed, willing him to breathe. He had alerted the clinic's security to be especially aware of anyone showing unusual interest in the young patient. Usually they were tasked with keeping the patients from getting out. Watching for citizens potentially breaking in was a nice change for them.

Back in normal clothing, the Sojourner was happy to be leaving the city. The robe and hood were useful but hot and confining. He regretted losing the followers who had jumped to protect him, and he commended their loyalty, sang their praises to the small group who accompanied him. But he made it completely clear to them whose life was most important.

Dr. Ana Bede crossed her legs the other way and repeated yet again an explanation for Bartolo Bruxton of the portal between universes. She had given him this little lecture four or five times previously and each time he had not believed her. He thought if he asked her enough times, she would finally tell him the truth, his truth. For some reason, he was fascinated by the portal and wanted it to be a passageway to a garden of some kind.

The healer was, as usual when they had these conversations, agitatedly pacing and fooling with the string of amber beads he affected. Ana had come to realize that they were in fact some kind of meditation device. Once or twice a day he would return to the house at the beach where they were staying and retreat to his room where he would kneel and finger his beads, whispering some kind of repetitious verses which she could not understand.

The plot to create a fake abduction as a way to hide Ana was Bruxton's scheme. Through their affair, Teegan learned about his hidey-hole near the dead city and broached the idea of taking Ana there. Rather than having Ana "just disappear," Bruxton suggested the ruse. He advised telling no one at the villa, including Jordi and Colt. Ana refused to keep the plan from Colt. He would keep Jordi and the others from calling in the authorities.

Teegan claimed she would keep Jordi in the dark because he would worry. Ana assumed this nonsense was because Teegan was bored with Jordi and hoping to have some adventures with the healer. Teegan lived for adventure.

When they fled the bathhouse, Teegan laughed

and told her that Bart would try to persuade her to accept his beliefs. He had not done so, at least so far, perhaps because he felt her hatred. He had continually apologized for having to kill Teegan. He had cared for Teegan, he insisted. He even told her that Teegan had gone to a better place. Although, he had added, she had been a bad citizen while alive, it was her good luck to be killed for the cause. Because of this martyrdom she would now be in the garden.

Ana found the talk about gardens confusing. You grew vegetables in gardens, even, sometimes, flowers. This healer seemed obsessed with the idea of gardens.

Why would someone so obsessed with gardens have to kill Teegan, Ana had asked, sobbing. Her tears upset the healer who tried ineffectually to hush her. Because, he had said, the Sojourner ordered it.

What Sojourner, Ana had asked. She was not familiar with the term. The fat healer smiled beatifically and told her she would see, soon. The Sojourner was a traveler, on a mission. The Sojourner would be in the dead city soon.

What Sojourner? Ana had insisted. Was he a man or something supernatural?

She would see, soon.

She gave up.

Later, in her room, Ana wished she had the nerve to kill herself. She could walk out into the desert that surrounded the dead city and be killed by wild animals or die of dehydration. Let them discover the truth about the portal. Let them open another one if that was what they wanted. She smiled grimly to herself. It would be difficult, but it could be done. She didn't think they would want to, when they found out what it was.

Closing the portal was another story. She had been working feverishly on that problem since before she was kidnapped by Bruxton. She had spent the recent days in Deep Cove working from memory to reimagine and recreate the protocols. After all, her work had provided Elvistine with the final key; he had created the theory, but she had provided the crucial mathematics. In any case, and to buy time, she had been insisting to Bruxton that she needed Elvistine's notes from the institute. Despite being a sanctioned healer, he seemed to be a scientific illiterate,

The knowledge of the portal had broken Elvistine; she was no longer confident it would not break her. Knowing what it would do, she had begun to wonder whether she should not just open another one. The unknown Sojourner citizen seemed determined to use it for some nefarious religionist purpose, something strongly opposed to the guidance of the Conclave. Maybe when he understood the reality it would serve his purposes, for a while. In the overall scheme of things, it didn't matter.

Ana had never thought much about the Conclave. The elders had educated her and supported the institute. She had assumed their decrees were correct; nothing they did interfered in her life in any way. They were strongly opposed to religionism, but she wasn't a religionist herself so it didn't matter to her. Previously she had been too busy to worry about the threat religionists could pose. Now that she had been kidnapped by Bruxton, she began to see the wisdom of the Conclave's prohibitions.

When she wasn't working on her calculations, she

hated the idleness, being kept a prisoner. It gave her too much time to think about things other than the portal problem. She found herself thinking about Colt, about his strength and loyalty. She had taken him for granted, done nothing as they grew apart. Now she yearned to see him again, if only for a moment. She would apologize.

At least she could do what he would do. Tomorrow, when the healer headed into the dead city on his mysterious task, Ana would do some exploring. She hated violence, hearing Colt talk about his cage fighting bouts made her queasy, but after she got the lay of the land, and depending on what she found, she would cold cock the healer with one of the cast iron skillets from the kitchen and escape in his aircar.

21

Piet strode into the space in front of his trailer, wondering whether to expect trouble from the soldiers who had made camp there for the past day or so. This was the cadre he was expected to lead to the Sojourner, and he had failed. He could live with that.

Colt hung back in the doorway, watching for developments. A dozen soldiers were scattered around the space killing time playing cards, dozing, and fiddling with their weapons. A couple were practicing some kind of martial art that piqued his interest.

The commander and one of her lieutenants had taken over the table that always sat in front of Piet's trailer and were playing a board game. The game consisted of a piece of silk embroidered with a pattern of some kind and various colored pebbles. When Piet approached, she immediately stood up, sweeping the game pieces into the piece of silk. She bowed slightly then held out her hand to fist bump. Colt noticed her insignia was unlike the one he had taken from the dead stalker.

"Citizen Lem," she spoke with a slight pleasant accent. "Are you here to lead us to the target?"

"I am not. We were attacked and the target fled." He matter-of-factly looked at his trailer.

"Where is the young citizen who was staying in my home?" he asked.

She looked surprised.

"When we arrived, I examined the inside of your home to ensure that no one hostile to ourselves was inside, but it was empty."

Piet gestured for Colt to join them then wearily sank into one of the chairs. After introducing Colt, he described the ambush and the resulting injury to his son.

"So none of the Sojourner's bodyguards escaped." The commander sounded skeptical.

"I don't think the citizens who attacked us could be described as bodyguards. They were too undisciplined and unskilled. They did their best, but it was wholly inadequate. The Sojourner, if that is truly the citizen in the robe, is obviously trained and he is the one who threw the dagger that wounded my son."

"I'm sorry about your son," she sounded perfunctory. "Do you have any idea where the Sojourner has fled to?"

Piet mentioned the name the dying religionist had uttered, but no one could identify it.

The commander turned and spoke a few words in an unsanctioned tongue and as a result the soldiers began gathering up their equipment. Colt wandered over and chatted with one of the marital artists. The citizen was friendly but barely fluent in the sanctioned tongue. After describing the basics of the art she practiced, she told Colt this group of soldiers was on loan to the C.E. from a warlord who commanded a large area in a distant land. She said, with pride, that she was part of a cadre who were specially trained to infiltrate and perform assassinations, kidnappings, sabotage, and the like. Since they had arrived in the Subs nothing had happened so they were looking forward to getting some action. She had not personally been told anything about the target. In answer to Colt's questions, she replied that, oh yes, they did see a lot of action. The C.E. was always borrowing them for one thing and another. There was a lot of unrest.

The commander handed Piet a comm. "For the time being and until we receive further orders, we will return to our main camp in the Subs. Here is a comm you may use to contact me at any time."

"I had heard that you took some casualties in the bombing," Piet said. "I assume you were searching for the Sojourner on your own. Or was it a different mission."

The commander could not be drawn. "This is difficult terrain," she said, looking him in the eye, "even for you."

They coolly fist bumped and the soldiers silently exited the cavern, leaving it as if they had never been there.

Piet made a call and a tray of food and tea appeared. He continued making calls while Colt ate and wishing Arlo would hurry back with intel about the dead city. The high authority was not happy with Piet.

After they ate, Colt accompanied Piet to the clinic

where Beau had been transported. Looking grave, Yonatan reported that his condition was unchanged. As they were leaving one of the attendants remarked that the healer had not left the patient's side since he was admitted.

Later, after Colt left for the House of Blue Leaves, Piet met with various members of Grupo Uno to try to find out what the heck was going on in the Subs. He also hoped to find Rowan and identify who had taken her from his trailer. He didn't think she would have recovered quickly from the soporific patch on her neck so someone had to come get her, carry her out. Piet would visit her guardian as his first task.

When Colt returned to Sparrow's to get some sleep, the House of Blue Leaves was back in business. The official lockdown had not been lifted, but life was getting back to normal in the city. Comm lines were working and the food kiosks on which most city dwellers relied for food were back in operation.

He couldn't sleep though. After a much-needed sonic shower, he wandered over to the massage room and had a deep-tissue treatment. After that, he was physically so relaxed he could barely make it back to his room. But his mind wouldn't shut up. It kept reminding him that his life was in turmoil. He thought back to the time when he was deciding to retire from the military and quit cage fighting. After a while, he had come to hate moving from place to place all the time. The fighting was okay; he was good at it and he liked it. He hadn't liked the hero-worship the C.E. encouraged toward athletes. He knew he was not a hero; cage fighting meant keeping in shape, staying fit and, most importantly, being willing to be hurt.

So he had returned to the city and settled down with Ana. He had plenty of money. Ana had plenty of money. They had a nice flat and good times with Teegan and Jordi.

He groaned and rolled over, feeling unaccustomed tears in his eyes. Teegan was dead and not only that but brutally strangled. He hoped the killer had been kind enough to make it quick; he was a healer after all. Jordi was falling apart. Getting shotgunned and almost dying had unmanned him. It did that to some people, Colt knew, and Jordi was not a fighter, not, ultimately, strong.

Ana was gone. Somehow he didn't think she was in real danger—yet. They needed her for something.

But someone was also looking for him. That made no sense at all. He knew nothing, had no skills other than cage fighting and gambling, was not rich. Maybe they thought they could use him to force Ana to do something. He laughed to himself. He could be crucified upside down with his blood dripping on her face and she wouldn't do anything she didn't want to. He loved that about her.

This all began when Arlo came back to the city. It figured. Arlo was the center of the cyclone.

Colt swore and reached for the bedside comm. Maybe a blowjob would push him over the edge, and he could get some shuteye. When the young postulant showed up a couple of minutes later, full of anticipation because Colt was much admired, Colt suddenly just wanted to talk. He asked a lot of questions, listening to the kid's soft answers. I'm getting old, he thought, this kid is half my age. He was losing his edge. Gaming no longer thrilled him and he wanted comfort more than sex. Swell, he thought, pulling the kid close and falling asleep.

Refreshed, Colt was hanging out in the cafe playing backgammon with one of the kids and working his way through a pile of sweetmeats when Arlo returned. He slouched into the room, obviously tired and hung over, avid for news; his dark beard and hair were inappropriately long. The citizens in the whiskey commune had welcomed him with open arms and open bottles. Business was brisk for them and news from the outside in short supply. No one believed the official videos about the explosion in the city. Several hundred people had died and the formal version was that radical religionists were building bombs and blew themselves up.

That sent two messages, Arlo thought. The religionists were stupid and no one wanted them living next door.

The kid went to get Arlo tea and while Arlo began working on the sweetmeats, Colt filled him in on the fight with the Sojourner's followers and Beau's injury.

"He did it on purpose, you think?" Arlo mused. Adding, "He knew you?"

"He knew Piet and Beau. Whether he knew me or not, I can't say. But, yes, it looked intentional. He could have as easily killed Beau outright."

Arlo called the Sojourner a few names.

"There's more."

Colt told Arlo that Piet thought he recognized the Sojourner. He mentioned the name.

"Boxes within boxes," Arlo said, leaving Colt puzzled.

Colt then told Arlo the name that the dying religionist had uttered. The name no one recognized.

"Oh," Arlo said. "I know that name. It's the old name of the dead city. See, I got a map."

He spread a map on the table between them. It had been transferred onto a silky material from a paper map back when citizens were told paper sheltered a deadly virus. While the details were fuzzy, the main outlines of the city were clear.

"My contact says there has been a lot of activity in the area lately. The guys in the commune no longer rely on dead cities to recover stashes of old liquor, but some of them would occasionally snoop around, as a kind of hobby, looking for valuable items to put on the collectors' market. They've quit that for the time being in the dead city. In the past, the authorities had apparently stopped paying attention to the odd tramp or vagrant. A few citizens wandering around in the city didn't bother them, but the surveillance satellites have been spending more time in the area lately.

"Interestingly, the dead city used to be the site of an important Conclave laboratory. In fact, the huge desert that stretches beyond the city was reputed to be unlivable as a result of research experiments. The guys in the whiskey commune report seeing a few large animals moving into the area so anyone who explores there needs to be heavily armed."

Arlo stretched and drank some tea. "I take it you are going to the dead city."

Colt nodded. "And once Piet hears that the Sojourner is headed there, he will want to go too."

"Can you get in touch with your buddies in the commune and ask them some questions?"

"Just as soon as I get a bath and a shave."

"Good," Colt suddenly felt invigorated at the idea of action. "I have a plan."

Piet was watching his son and Yonatan through a window at the clinic. An attendant had urged him not to waken them. Beau was no longer in a coma; he was just sleeping. And Yonatan, who had not left his side, had fallen asleep in his chair, still holding Beau's hand.

"You son should be fine," the attendant said briskly, "but it will be a long recovery."

"It looks like he's in good hands," Piet said, without irony.

"The best."

Colt had called with the news that Arlo was back and had identified the name mentioned by the religionist as that of the dead city.

22

That evening Colt, Arlo, and Piet met at Sparrow's for a council of war. Sparrow gave them a corner of the cafe and joined them, at their request. Servers brought a succession of delectable small plates and Sparrow was free with his favorite retsina. He was upset about Beau's terrible injury, he liked the young citizen and had frequently, with Piet's amused consent, comped him services.

Arlo had spent an enjoyable afternoon in the House spa and was again clean-shaven, his thick curly hair for the moment subdued. After toasting the elders and getting an update on Beau's condition—which was stable and Yonatan was optimistic—Arlo pushed the dishes aside and spread the map of the dead city on the table.

In its day, it had been quite extensive, built along the coast. It was mainly a resort area with many hotels and fine summer homes for wealthy families from nearby cities. The map revealed an organized plan with streets radiating from a central square. Several smaller squares with churches, museums, an opera house, and a central market were all indicated on the map. A cluster of buildings on the outskirts was labeled Laboratory and another large building farther out was merely labeled Refinery without further explanation. Docks and marinas were arrayed along the coast with a large amusement park on a big pier extending into the water.

He looked at the intent faces around him and pointed to the pier. "I asked my guys at the commune, per Colt's request, whether the spy satellites typically flew over the water. They said they didn't think the satellites functioned well over water. They said, as far as they knew, no one went anywhere near the water other than a few crazy fishermen because it was so dangerous."

They all looked at Colt, who said, with gusto, "Look, the dead city is not that far up the coast from Deep Cove. If we take one or more aircars and start toward the dead city, we may—make that, almost certainly will—attract attention either from the authorities or from the parties that are using the dead city as a hideout. If the Sojourner is really going to the dead city, he isn't going alone and for the sightseeing. Something is going on there. They may have their own eyes in the sky. My idea would be to go to Deep Cove, which should not attract much attention, and make a deal with one of the local fishermen to take us up the coast."

Arlo was not surprised at this plan, given Colt's question to the communards, and Piet looked thoughtful.

Before anyone could speak, the kid who was topping off the retsina glasses, piped up, "Oh, you can't possibly go on a boat, on the water. Everyone knows it's too dangerous; the water is full of aggressive mutant water spiders and leviathans. Oh, Colt, be careful." He looked at them in horror.

Sparrow pulled the teenager onto his lap. "My kids are so fond of Colt," he said to the table. Turning to the kid, he patted him on the knee. "It's time for you to take a break. Grab a bottle of wine and go to my studio. I'll be along shortly."

The kid hopped up, smiling, and hurried away, but Piet thought there was some concern in his eyes. Sparrow ran a tight ship.

Ignoring the byplay, Colt continued, "We can pick up Jordi on the way." He had not mentioned his concerns about Jordi's mental health to his friends. Still he knew Jordi would want to accompany them to avenge Teegan if not for the adventure.

"What about that Oren citizen?" Piet asked. "He's still living with Rick and Ilsa while Linnet helps Ilsa." They all grinned at this white lie. Linnet would be doing all the housework and waiting on Ilsa. "He looked like he might be a good man in a fight and he's used to the countryside. My guys in Grupo Uno would be lost outside the city." Even if I could trust them, he thought bitterly.

Colt explained about Oren's religionism but, like Linnet, Piet and Arlo were underwhelmed. "Lot of religionists walking around," Arlo spoke for them. "As long as they keep it to themselves, its not a problem. Look at it this way, we would be doing Rick and Ilsa a favor."

The meeting broke up. Piet went to personally check on Beau. Arlo rolled up the map of the dead city and went back to his room to make some calls now that the comm frequencies were open.

Sparrow remained, sipping retsina. Colt enjoyed his company. The older man had a wealth of experience; he had not been the manager of a sex club forever. And he had insight.

"What do you think about approaching the dead city from the water side?" Colt asked.

Sparrow considered. "I think it could work. I have not had a lot of experience on the coast, but I doubt the sea creatures are as dangerous as my little postulant thinks. Large sections of the waters, like large sections of the land, were essentially dead from pollution before the plague. I've been told that animals are returning to many previously contaminated lands so why not to the water, as well. Animals were not as affected by the plague; they may have contributed by carrying the plague, they may not. Part of your problem will be finding a water rat who knows the coast and is willing to take a chance. There may be some smuggling going on that draws the attention of the authorities. Personally, I think it's worth a try."

Colt decided to confide in Sparrow. "I'm having mixed feelings about bringing Piet and Arlo to the dead city. I think it would be easier for me to ghost around there without detection than with either of them. Arlo is not and never has been a warrior. He's a thinker, and, maybe not such a good thinker."

"Do you trust him?"

Colt shrugged. "I've known him a long time." Not wanting to go there. He continued, "Piet is too emotionally involved. Piet let us walk into that ambush in the Subs, it was his territory and the toothless wraiths in the Subs were his toothless wraiths. I'm not comfortable putting all the responsibility for our discovery on the motion sensor in the tunnel. Maybe it's just a retired soldier's paranoid survivalist instinct, but I think we were probably sold out by one of his Sub rats."

"Also," Sparrow said judiciously, "Now that Beau is badly injured, will Piet want to leave?"

Colt shrugged.

"I'm always wary of citizens looking for vengeance. It can lead to recklessness and bad judgment."

Colt didn't mention that Jordi's need to avenge Teegan would present the same problems. His mental instability would complicate matters.

"I can't tell him not to go. And he's a good citizen in a fight. Meanwhile my agenda is clear. I want to find Ana and get her to safety. Then I'll worry about revenging Beau and Teegan."

"Anything I can do to assist, citizen Bede, let me know," Sparrow started to rise but Colt said, "As a matter of fact, I have an idea."

Sparrow was all ears. He listened avidly to Colt's request then waddled off to have a few words with the chatty kid.

23

In Deep Cove, the atmosphere in Rick and Ilsa's villa had become almost unbearably tense. Ilsa spent her days in her room, worrying that the authorities would find out about Oren and that the murderer, whoever it was, who had brutally killed someone so close to her, might be coming for her, for them. Rick had taken her away from the stresses of the city, and she had spent the last ten years with him, secure and cared for. There had been the brief uproar with Irene Thorne, but, when it was over, they were alone again. Then Linnet had taken the remaining household chores off her shoulders as well as nursing Rick and Jordi. Life was almost perfect. Now invisible forces threatened her sanctuary.

She spent time with Jordi. Only he really understood how she felt. Linnet and even Rick thought she was overreacting to Oren's religionism. As long as he didn't share his beliefs with anyone in the little village, they would be safe. She didn't trust him. She didn't consort with him, of course. Even had he not been infected with unsanctioned beliefs, he was quite uncouth. Thankfully, he stayed away from her, spending most of his days tinkering with the aircar and running errands for Linnet and Rick.

Ilsa and Jordi were sitting on the topmost terrace, sipping from a carafe of sweet wine. Rick was locked in his room, reading from his small stash of secret books, and Linnet was somewhere doing household chores. From their vantage point, they could see Oren tinkering with the aircar.

Ilsa was distraught, her beautiful eyes ravaged from lack of sleep. "I can't make Rick understand the danger, Jordi. All he wants to do is hide in his room studying his books." She said the final word with loathing. "It never bothered me before, books are dangerous and unsanctioned but nothing like harboring a religionist, especially, one who follows," she dropped her voice, "the Man in the Sky.

"Now Rick just hides from me all the time. He and Linnet insist no one in the village knows about Oren's unsanctioned beliefs, but you know how these people are, they are compelled to bring other people over to their way of thinking. Once he tries that, they will turn him in and our lovely little sanctuary will be gone, we'll have to move. Who knows what will happen to us. Do you think we can convince them that we are loyal to the Conclave of Elders? What are we going to do?"

Jordi looked ravaged, himself. He was still thin and pale; he kept running his long fingers through his hair so that it stood out around his head in disarray. His golden curls had faded to a dirty beige. Now, he stared moodily at Oren as he bent over the aircar, remembering him kneeling beside Teegan's dead body. "I don't know what the authorities will believe. They are corrupt themselves. Irene Thorne had their protection."

Ilsa gripped her wineglass, "No one knows what Irene Thorne wanted other than little Linnet and poor dear Desmond Elvistine. He was always such a quiet man, even when he came to university parties, he never talked to anyone except Ana and Menard Tillman, before Menard was sent away."

She shuddered gracefully. "I still have nightmares about the helicopter descending out of nowhere, deafening, and the guns . . ." She drank some wine and tears came to her eyes.

Jordi stopped staring into space and reached over, touching her hand awkwardly. He didn't really know what to do to comfort her. Teegan had never cried or showed any kind of weakness. Ilsa was so different, so beautiful and pitiful.

"It will be okay," he said. "We'll figure something out."

"We must send him away."

"Colt wants us to keep him here, where we can keep an eye on him."

Ilsa jumped up and started pacing. Her beautifully trained voice rang vibrant with distress. "How long before Colt returns? When will he be back? I expect he's off somewhere looking for his wife. He doesn't care about us. Why should he?" More tears fell and Jordi moved beside her, patting her shoulder. He felt terrible bitterness and rage at the downward spiral his life had become. He kept envisioning everything that had happened: being terribly wounded, losing Teegan, Ana going missing, and now this lovely, fragile woman's life being threated by a religionist.

"Try not to worry," he whispered. "We'll be okay." Holding her while she cried.

24

Ana had decided to channel her husband, to throw off her prisoner's lethargy, and begin viewing Bruxton not as a misguided religionist but as the enemy. She drank coffee, maintained her usual routine, waiting for him to leave. He left, stopping, as usual, to lock the doors. He is stupid, she thought, as if she couldn't easily break one of the many windows. She began a systematic search of the cottage.

Among other things—communications devices, weapons—she was looking for a map. The cottage was small and square with terraces at the front and back. It had probably been a vacation cottage, there was little storage. A dilapidated shed in the back yard held bags of lawn care supplies and rusty implements.

In the cottage, the appliances and furniture were new but she found a small pantry with miscellaneous junk, old dishes and glassware, cutlery, pots and pans, and, because the owners must have ignored the order to destroy everything printed on paper, three cookbooks and an ancient comm directory. As a scientist, Ana didn't really believe in the paper virus, but she handled the old book with her hands encased in a handy pair of washing-up gloves. Opening the brittle pages carefully, she briefly wished she had a respirator, she found a central section with a schematic map of the dead city. The book was falling to pieces as she handled it, however carefully, so she quickly drew the map on her tablet. Jordi would have been so useful here; he would have drawn it perfectly to scale and with all the details in half the time it took her.

As she continued pilfering through the cottage, she found some other surprising items. The kitchen had an assortment of knives and a sharpening block. Apparently Bruxton didn't think of a razor-sharp chef's knife as a weapon for chopping anything other than vegetables.

And, bingo, searching Bruxton's bedroom, she found, ineptly hidden, a conventional pistol, clean and fully loaded. Suspecting a trap, she looked around but saw nothing that could be a surveillance device. She quickly unloaded the pistol, glad she had too often watched Colt fool with his weapons. She thought about getting rid of the bullets somehow, then decided they might come in handy. She had never shot a pistol, but how hard could it be?

In the shallow closet in her bedroom she found a hidden compartment in the floor opening onto a cache of old photographs, pictures of pre-plague families, parents and children together, and lots of small animals. Ana shuddered at a picture of a fat baby laughing as it lay propped up against a large black dog. She thought the dog had a kind of grin on its face, too. So dangerous those animals had been and the people never knew. She remembered stories about people actually dying protecting their companion animals from the authorities.

Ilsa had kept that ugly cat around the villa back in Deep Cove, swearing that it had been tested and was safe. That memory set Ana to wondering what was going on in Deep Cove, if anyone knew that Teegan was dead. She had been painting a picture in her mind of Bruxton as a bumbler, leaving her alone in a house she could easily escape from, leaving behind sharp knives and a loaded pistol hidden at the back of a drawer. But he had quickly and efficiently strangled Teegan; Ana had watched in horror, unable to act until it was too late. Then afraid he would kill her next, tried to run before he quickly tied her hands together. She should remember there were two sides to Bartolo Bruxton.

Conversely, she smiled to herself; he apparently thought she wasn't dangerous.

She returned the photos to their hiding place under the floor. Maybe they harbored the paper virus and she was going to die soon; that didn't make her feel sad. If someone didn't find a way to close the portal, they were all going to die soon. She was sad because all the dead people in the pictures had looked so happy.

Colt left for Deep Cove the next morning, having convinced Piet and Arlo to let him go first and reconnoiter. Arlo was reluctant to stay in the city, but Piet didn't argue, eager to stay close to Beau. Because they had sent Rick's aircar back to the villa, Colt borrowed one of Piet's vehicles. He had no trouble passing through the checkpoints that encircled the city since the lockdown because the bored guards were just not paying attention. Commercial traffic was now moving freely and the occasional private aircar was waved through without a glance.

He briefly considered stopping at the clinic to determine whether healer Bruxton had reappeared or been in contact with any of the staff, but opted to hurry on to Deep Cove. He left the aircar outside the village and approached the villa on foot. Rick was standing outside the front gate talking to a representative of the local authority. When he saw Colt, Rick looked greatly relieved.

"Thank you, citizen, for your interest in our problems. I see my wife's cousin from the city is approaching. He's come to be with us during this terrible time."

The cop turned cop's eyes on Colt.

"Citizen," he said.

Colt nodded pleasantly and held out a fist.

The cop reluctantly fist bumped.

"Where's your aircar," he looked behind Colt.

"I caught a ride with a friend," Colt said.

"Someone down for the festival?" the cop said. "I thought the city was on lockdown."

"That seems to be pretty much over," Colt looked at Rick. "I should go see Ilsa."

The cop stepped aside and watched Colt go through the gate.

"He looks familiar," he said to Rick.

Rick said nothing and the cop assured him they would be back later to question Ilsa, when she was able to talk.

Ilsa was sitting in the dark living room, her face

buried in her hands. When Colt spoke her name, she jerked upright, spitting out the words,

"You, why weren't you here? You could have stopped him. I told him you didn't care about us."

"Who?" Colt asked quietly, throwing his backpack on the floor, and seating himself beside her, trying to take her hand.

"Jordi. Jordi's gone. He killed them. He killed them and he left."

Colt shook his head, stunned.

"Who did he kill? Who did Jordi kill?"

"Linnet and Oren." Rick spoke as he returned to the room. "He shot them both."

"Linnet?" Colt was gobsmacked. "Why Linnet?"

"We're not sure." Rick was clearly exhausted. "We think he killed her because he thought she was becoming a religionist like Oren."

"Was she?" Colt asked.

"I don't think so. She thought it was silly. Dangerous and silly. She remonstrated with Oren all the time, urging him to be silent on the topic, reminding him how he could put us all in danger."

"What happened then?"

"Jordi was becoming more and more unstable. He was obsessed with the danger Oren presented to us." Rick gave Ilsa a hard look as he said this. "My wife encouraged him."

"I was terrified that he would do something stupid, try to convert someone, and the authorities would blame us for harboring him." Ilsa held a shredded handkerchief to her face.

"Jordi came upon Linnet and Oren, in their room, kneeling. Maybe they were acting religionist or maybe they were looking for something they dropped on the floor. Apparently seeing them in that way triggered his rage because he went to his room, got his gun, and shot both of them."

Colt remembered the scene in the artifact storage when Jordi had seen Oren kneeling over Teegan's body.

"Where is he now?"

"Gone. To the dead city. He took my aircar and fled."

Colt stood up, stretched, anxious to move.

"Why the dead city? Did he have a reason?" It made a kind of immediate sense, to go somewhere like the dead city where there might be a place to hide. But why wouldn't Jordi flee back to the city, to the Subs. Piet would hide him, protect him from the authorities. Colt knew he was not thinking clearly; he was shaken over Linnet's death, little Linnet as Sparrow had called her.

Rick was speaking. "He was going to find the healer who killed Teegan. He said you thought the healer had taken Ana to the dead city."

25

It was imperative that Colt get to the dead city as soon as possible. He needed to find Ana, but he needed to get Jordi to safety, too. Jordi was not, anymore, someone who could take care of himself, especially not in unfamiliar territory. Colt could see Jordi going off half-cocked and getting himself killed. Colt didn't want to lose more friends.

It was also imperative that he act soon. Rick said the authorities seemed to have taken them at their word that they had not known that Oren and Linnet were religionists. They had glanced cursorily at the bedrooms used by Oren and Linnet and Jordi. They had not shown any interest in Rick's study where he kept his unsanctioned paper books or in the rest of the house. Rick and Ilsa told them Oren and Linnet were employees and that Jordi, an old friend from the university, had been distraught because his wife had run away with someone else. Was the other citizen a religionist? the officer had asked. They had replied— yes, yes, how did you know?—and the officer had smirked and said it figured.

Rick didn't think they would expend too much effort trying to find Jordi unless, that is, the authorities who had taken Oren's and Linnet's bodies away, discovered she had been pregnant. Killing a pregnant woman, even a religionist, was a serious crime. If they discovered Linnet had been pregnant, they would conduct an actual investigation.

Rick also pointed out that because the village was small there was no local authority; any necessary policing was done out of a small city down the coast. Villagers themselves handled most petty crime that happened. They were very insular, and he was skeptical that Colt could get any of the water rats to take him to the dead city.

Later that night found Colt at the bar in the tavern where he and Jordi had hung out previously. It was not the only bar in town, but it was the seediest, and located along the shore. Looking carefully from his bar stool through the open sides of the shack, Colt could make out ghost lights far out on the water.

The bartender had greeted Colt like an old friend, sliding a hefty bourbon his way. He wanted to mine Colt for nuggets of gossip, and Colt was more than willing to be mined.

"Ever find that girlfriend of yours what walked out on you?" he initiated the conversation.

"Nope," Colt savored his drink. "You didn't see her around here, did you?"

"Nope, nor your friend's girl neither." He paused, "I heard she run away with a religionist," he ventured.

"That's what they say."

"That's what pushed your buddy over the edge,

like."

"I guess so." Colt sighed, sadly. "Did you know the couple working for my cousin and her husband were religionists?"

"We don't get too many religionists in here," the bartender grinned. Two of his teeth were capped with silver.

"I expect not," Colt signaled for another drink.

"They think your buddy walked into the water."

"Who thinks that?"

"The cop who came up to investigate came in for a quick one. He said that's what he would do. He said your buddy was kind of crazy."

"Was he basing that on some fact or just speculating?"

"Don't know. He was annoyed that he had to transport the bodies to the crematorium. He was pissing and moaning that they should buy him a fusion pistol so he could just disappear citizens' bodies."

"Fusion pistols are hard to come by," Colt said.

"They're expensive, anyway," the bartender said, meaningfully.

Okay, Colt thought. The bartender might have a few less-than-sanctioned sidelines.

"There seems to be quite a lot of things going on up at their villa, the professor and his young girlfriend. Someone claimed they saw a helicopter. That would be Conclave business."

"I doubt that. The professor just got tired of life in the city. He enjoys the seaside."

The bartender nodded and polished some glasses. After a few minutes, Colt said, "It seems quiet tonight."

"It's early. The boys will be coming in soon."

"What do you do around here? Fish?" Colt said, indifferently. "I thought the water was dangerous."

"Not if you know what you're doing. Most of the locals have lived here forever. They grew up in boats. The water's okay. You don't want to swim in it, but some of the fish are edible. Mostly they keep the catch for themselves and sell some of it at the market."

"You're not a fisherman yourself?"

"Nope. I'm from down south. Came here in the military and just stayed. I like it here. It's close to the city but not too close, if you know what I mean."

The bartender went to wait on another customer. The crowd was starting to drift in.

When he returned, Colt said, "I heard there was a festival going on. Anything exciting happening?"

"It depends on what excites you. It is mostly aircar races on the beach. Citizens come from the city; there's some wagering, if that excites you."

Colt had to admit, that aspect of it did excite him.

"Citizens will start arriving tomorrow. Probably a smaller crowd than usual because of the lockdown in the city."

"A couple of friends of mine might enjoy aircar races. Is it too late to get a place to stay?" The bartender assured him he could fix them up.

Colt thought it was time to move the agenda on.

"I'm not too interested in aircar races, but I would like to go for a boat ride. I've always thought it would be an adventure," he said. He was ready to elaborate, but it was unnecessary.

"If you've got the ready cash, you might talk to Old Matley. He's got a little boat; says he used to go up to the dead city hunting artifacts, back in the day."

The bartender directed him to a couple of citizens at a table in a corner almost hidden by a hanging plant. The two were dressed in the heavy denim favored by the locals; both wore earrings and kerchiefs covering their hair. A denim cap lay on the table and a bottle and two glasses of some fluorescent green liquid rested nearby. After giving the bartender a healthy tip and ordering another round for himself and the couple, Colt wandered over.

The male citizen looked unfriendly even after the bartender brought over another carafe. The female citizen stared at the table.

"You want something?" Old Matley said.

Colt took a seat and looked at the companion.

"She don't talk. She had an accident with her tongue."

Colt thought about this for a minute.

"I'm sorry to hear that," he said.

He paused for a minute, sizing them up.

"I have some old money I need to get rid of."

"Who would we have to kill?" the citizen asked.

"Nothing like that. I have a hankering to take a boat ride," he said. "The bartender tells me you have a boat."

"Why?"

"I've always been drawn to adventure." The female rat glanced up at this. She had an accident with her teeth, too.

Old Matley grinned. "Where you want to go on this adventure?" he asked.

"I understand there's a dead city up the coast. I've always wanted to explore one of those."

"A kind of double adventure, huh. A boat ride and

exploring a dead city. Might be expensive." He swilled some of his drink, which smelled as bad as it looked.

Colt laid a large bill on the table.

"You got some more of those?"

"A few."

Colt's new best friend said, "The authorities frown on citizens exploring dead cities."

"They have no sense of adventure. I've heard that the authorities generally don't send their spy satellites over the water," Colt said.

"That's right. No citizen in their right mind is on the water and no one alive is in it. But the authorities might not be your only problem with this dead city." Now that he had seen Colt's money, he was more forthcoming. "There are quite a few unfriendly citizens there."

"You mean squatters?"

"No, I mean citizens with automatic weapons who look like they know what to do with them." But Old Matley didn't know much about them, like where they were from. They were not in uniform but they carried themselves like trained troops. When questioned he said he could not tell whether they spoke an unsanctioned tongue because he never got that close to them. They looked normal, he said, by which Colt inferred they were not from the land of volcanoes or other foreign shores.

As kids, Old Matley explained, he and his friends used to explore the dead city. They would take boats up and snoop around, looking for cool stuff. Then most of them, himself included, had got busy making a living, and he had not gone up that way for years. A few folks—artifact hunters mostly—had maintained an interest in the dead city and reports had started filtering through that strangers had moved in. Maybe they were authorized to be there. No one got close enough to ask before they started shooting. Reportedly they were doing something at the old lab and generating plant.

"Tell me about the generating plant?" Arlo's map had labels reading merely Refinery and Laboratory. Old Matley explained that the dead city had employed hundreds of citizens in a facility that turned algae grown in vast ponds outside the city into fuel to be used for generating power. No one had been able to get close enough to find out what they were using the power for now. One of the interested parties, with some knowledge of engineering, thought that, based on the amount of algae they were cultivating, they were planning to generate quite a lot of power.

No one knew what they were doing at the lab, neither. About the lab, which was in close proximity to the refinery and generating plant, Old Matley knew only that it had once been operated by the Conclave of Elders.

There were, he said, abandoned cottages and villas all along the coast beginning not too far from their village and extending past the dead city for several klicks. Beyond the last house was a vast empty prairie which, before the plague, had been uninhabitable because of pollution from, what Old Matley termed, bad air. Now it was home to wild animals, big cats and wolf creatures.

A few citizens who didn't care for company squatted in the abandoned buildings at the outer edges.

"Maybe someone's planning to make the dead city live again," Colt suggested.

"Maybe." The water rat was not convinced.

But, he had added, generously, if Colt wanted to divest himself of some of the old money that was weighing him down, and go adventuring in the dead city, he was the citizen to provide a helping hand.

They continued chatting for a few minutes. Old Matley advised that comms typically did not operate over the water; he couldn't speak to whether they would operate in the dead city itself. They made an appointment to meet the next evening.

Old Matley's female companion said nothing, continuing to stare at her hands and drink glass after glass of the fluorescent beverage. They offered him a taste; it was unpleasantly herbal and caused him to see stars.

26

Chandler Besdine arrived in the dead city completely exhausted. He usually could continue pushing himself, going without sleep, for days, if necessary. Now he knew he needed to crash. The managers of the facility were anxious to see him. As the Conclave's representative, he was the boss; they were eager to show him how well they had followed directions, how successful they had been in achieving the goals of the project. He put them off, claiming fatigue.

His grandfather's suite of rooms, where he had lived and worked as the director of both the laboratory and refinery, was in the penthouse of the laboratory building immediately below the heliport. Toward the end of his life, his grandfather had spent most of his time there, with only brief excursions back to the Conclave's headquarters. The lab staff had been directed to prepare the space for Chandler's use, and he was happy to see they had complied. The rooms were clean, the bed made up.

In addition to exhaustion, he was starving. Before

anything else, though, he checked the safe, just to be sure no one had found it by accident. His grandfather's deathbed words had been mysterious to those present, but Chandler, knowing how the old personage thought, interpreted them and found the safe where he had hidden the directions for culturing the plague. When he found the safe hidden where he had expected, he had felt a surge of delight and love. When he read the letter left for him by his ancestor, he had been changed fundamentally and his life had been given purpose. He now felt euphoric because he was finally close to completing his ancestor's mission. After carefully closing the well-hidden safe, he used the lab comm to order some food from the kitchen and when it arrived, collapsed into a chair to eat. Then he slept.

In the city, Piet was standing with Yonatan looking down at Beau, who was once more in a coma, this one chemically induced. Yonatan was explaining the reasons for the treatment, but, although Piet was listening, he was not hearing. He was too aware of Beau's drawn, pale features. Always thin, he was almost skeletal now, and his hospital clothes looked unpleasantly like burial wrappings.

Yonatan looked pretty terrible, too. Pale and gaunt, he had obviously been keeping watch 24/7.

Piet had finally had an opportunity to describe for Yonatan what had gone down in the Subs under the protestors' camp. He had described the skillful way the robed one had thrown the dagger at Beau, intending, Piet was sure, to wound both of them. He had failed, Beau was alive, and now Piet was going to the dead city to annihilate the Sojourner and all his followers. He came from an ancient line that believed in visiting vengeance on the families and, if possible, the entire tribes of transgressors.

He did not mention to Yonatan his suspicions about the identity of the Sojourner. In fact, as he thought about the issue, he became less certain himself. The role seemed out of character for the citizen he had in mind. Ultimately it did not matter. The Sojourner was a dead citizen, whoever he was.

Piet said, "I heard from Colt. He's gone ahead to Deep Cove to reconnoiter. He found a mess when he got there. His friend Jordi had apparently gone crazy and killed the two kids who worked for Rick and Ilsa. Jordi has a thing about religionists. And apparently he has now gone to the dead city to avenge his wife, to find and kill the healer."

"Bruxton," Yonatan said grimly. "Does he know Bruxton is a religionist?"

"Not that I know of. I don't think he cares at this point. Colt says the authorities think he walked into the water and he, Rick, and Ilsa are letting them think that. Rick and Ilsa didn't mention the dead city idea to them. Ilsa, at least, is glad they are dead. I gather she was scared to death that the young citizen, Oren, would be exposed and she and Rick would suffer."

"I never met the citizens," Yonatan said, "but they are justified in worrying about harboring religionists. Those small villages are prone to vigilante justice. And the Conclave has been especially restive lately. Issuing directives and so forth."

He looked thoughtfully at Piet, then at Beau.

"I can't go with you to the dead city to pursue this Sojourner personage. My place is here with Beau." He gently stroked the boy's cheek.

He continued, "Candidly I wouldn't be much help if I did. However, I have something you may find use for. I never will."

He removed a small wooden jewel case from his medical bag and handed it to Piet.

"These are the treatment modalities, so described by the Elders, developed for incurable religionists. I believe they are instruments of terror, and, even if I have to break my oath to the Conclave, I could not bring myself to use them on another citizen, however misguided they were. I will make an exception for the Sojourner." He glanced over at Beau's unconscious form. "Take them and do what you will. The small item that looks like a cockroach must be within four to five centimeters of the target's body and must stay there for at least 45 minutes after it is triggered. The remote control can be farther away, several meters. Once the remote is triggered, the target will commit suicide within twenty four hours."

"Guaranteed?" Piet frowned.

"So the Elders say."

Piet looked at the diminutive, beautifully fashioned artifact and shuddered. But he put the box in his backpack.

"A personal directive from the Conclave accompanied the box. The devices are only for use on religionists, like the Sojourner. So if you use them on someone else, don't get caught."

27

Jordi zipped along the shore toward the dead city in Rick's aircar, using the program taken from the healer's charging station. He had no plans other than finding the healer and shooting him as he had Oren and Linnet. He truly regretted killing Linnet, but she had obviously been converted by Oren. Why else would they be kneeling in her bedroom? It was a religionist thing, kneeling.

It was fortunate for Jordi that the aircar was self-directed because he could barely see. His eyes were swollen and dry from sobbing and his vision was distorted by strange rainbow colors. Sounds too were unnecessarily loud and jarring. The shrieks of the birds overhead threatened and terrified him. They circled around him, yelling raucously, as though he were prey. He thought about shooting at them but he needed to save his ammunition for the healer.

The aircar began presently to pass more numerous cottages and occasionally a walled villa with beautifully wrought gates opening onto the beach. In the distance Jordi saw what looked like floating islands covered with black specks he took to be birds or sea animals.

At least, he thought, Ilsa would be safe now. The authorities would rightly blame him for killing the religionists but would, in all probability, not expend too much effort to find him. He had left a jacket and shoes on the shore below their villa, hoping they would assume he walked into the water.

The thought of the water touching him made him shudder, which caused his distorted vision to gyrate crazily.

Eventually he came to a section of the dead city that had once been commercial. The buildings were larger, even a few signs remained. The aircar slowed, as if looking for an address, which made him laugh wildly. He imagined the aircar as a flying animal, found himself looking out the side windows for wings.

The aircar sped up again and continued past what had been the center of the city, past a tumbledown amusement pier, toward more suburban cottages and villas. Within a short time, the aircar slowed once more and zipped to his left, away from the water, coming to rest in the garden behind a little cottage.

As he exited the aircar, holding his weapon before him, the back door of the small building opened. He raised the weapon, expecting to see the fat healer, anticipating his death, but instead, through his distorted gaze, he beheld Ana Bede, holding her hands in front of her to stop him shooting her.

He looked at her. Dazzled.

"Ana, it's you! Colt is coming to get you." He ran

toward her.

"Jordi," she looked wildly around. "Send the aircar somewhere. We can't let anyone see it."

He looked uncomprehending for a minute, then ran back to the aircar, recovering his backpack and setting the controls for the pre-programmed location near the artifact storeroom.

"Will you be able to get it back?" Ana asked, feeling an idiot.

Jordi grinned like a smart little boy, holding up the remote control.

Behind them, the aircar rose up a few feet and zipped out of sight.

Inside the cottage, Jordi gave Ana a big hug.

She was struck by how thin he had become in the short time since she had last seen him. He hurried feverishly through the four rooms of the small cottage. At last he said, "Where is the bastard, Bruxton? I expected him to be here."

"He's not here right now. I expect him shortly. He has a regular schedule. He works in some kind of lab in a distant part of the dead city." She looked anxiously through the window, then said, "Do you have a comm? We could call Colt."

Ana grabbed his arm eagerly as he handed her the comm, saying, "Give it a try. Communications have been working only intermittently since the lockdown in the city. They don't work well along the coast." They tried his comm unsuccessfully.

Ana followed Jordi into Bruxton's bedroom where he began looking through drawers and in the closet.

"What are you looking for?"

Instead of answering the question, Jordi said

casually, "I'm going to kill him."

"Why," Ana asked, although she thought she knew.

Her friend sagged onto a chair and put his hand in front of his face. "Teegan! I know she's dead, strangled. We found her body in the healer's artifact storage. He killed her. Bruxton killed her."

"I know," Ana said. "I was there. I think he's insane. His religionism has made him insane."

"So," Jordi said bitterly, "He's a religionist, too. We wondered why he kidnapped you."

"I don't think he kidnapped me just because he's a religionist. Something is going on at the laboratory. I think they need a scientist. "

Jordi looked interested. "What for?"

"That's what I want to find out. We need to keep trying the comm, but in the meantime we need to hide you."

"I want to kill Bruxton. I came to kill Bruxton. Then I'll be done." Jordi said stubbornly. "I don't need to hide."

Ana was adamant. "You can kill him later. I don't care if you do. I watched him strangle Teegan, and I couldn't do anything to save her. Still if we kill him now, we may attract attention and I don't want to do that . . . yet."

"Look, why do you care what they are doing in that lab?" Jordi tried to pull her toward the door. "Just wait here until Bruxton gets back, I'll shoot him, and we'll call the aircar and go back to the city. Colt and Piet can protect you in the city."

"No, I want to know what's going on here." Ana shook him off.

"Why? It's none of your business. It's probably

C.E. business and it's always a bad idea to get involved with them. You know that." He pleaded.

"I know that. I'm just curious, I guess."

Jordi gave up. Once Ana made up her mind, there was no moving her. He briefly thought about going ahead with his own plan, waiting for Bruxton to return, shooting him, and returning to Deep Cove to see Ilsa, and Rick, too, of course. What could Ana do to stop him?

But she was a very old friend, she needed him. And he very much feared she was in more danger than she knew.

28

Piet and Arlo had caught a ride with an aircar-racing aficionado. Before this, neither one had known that aircar racing existed, and they were both feeling a little stupid. On the trip to the village, the owner of the aircar explained in detail the intricacies of aircar racing. His own aircar was especially modified to be quicker and more maneuverable than ordinary vehicles, and they were soon sick of hearing about it. When they finally reached the village, they assured the citizen that they would bet heavily on him.

The streets were crowded with tourists, and no one looked twice at them. In fact, no authorities appeared to be present.

Although comm frequencies were still intermittent, they had managed earlier to reach Colt for a brief conversation. Colt told them about the bar and that the bartender would rent them lodging. Before he could tell them about the death of Oren and Linnet, the lines went dead.

The bartender, as he had promised, and in

exchange for some cash tokens, rented them a small cottage with two bedrooms behind the bar itself. It abutted a wooden pier to which numerous boats were tethered. The two city dwellers found the smell unpleasantly fishy.

Colt was at a table in the corner of the bar. Dressed in denim and a cap, he looked like he belonged with the male and female water rats seated next to him.

"Citizens," he stood and they fist bumped. "You made it." He motioned them to take seats and introduced them to Old Matley.

They ordered drinks and Arlo filled a few minutes regurgitating some of the factoids about aircar racing he had gleaned on the trip out from the city. Colt looked amused.

For old Matley's benefit, Piet said, "But why are you here? "I didn't think you cared for aircar racing."

"No, I'm here in Deep Cove because my cousin Ilsa and her partner Rick had a tragedy happen at their villa. I'm lending moral support. But while I'm here, I'm taking advantage of the opportunity to explore a dead city."

"I've always wanted to do that, myself," Piet said.

"These citizens are going to take me there by water in order to avoid the authorities' surveillance satellites."

"What was this tragedy at Rick and Ilsa's," Arlo butted in.

Colt kept his voice light, while looking meaningfully at Arlo.

"Their houseguest, who had been ill, had a breakdown and killed the two servants."

"Some breakdown," the male water rat muttered.

"Houseguest?" Arlo questioned.

"You remember Jordi Petrie from the university. He's been ill and, apparently, he found out the servants were committed religionists."

Arlo was in shock. Trying to control himself, he said, "It's been a while since I talked with Jordi."

He was going to ask more questions when Piet cut in, "We'll go up to the villa and offer our condolences."

Colt said gratefully, "You do that. Ilsa is very upset.

A waiter finally wandered over. Eyeing the two water rats' carafe of oily green liquid, Piet ordered another round for the table.

"On to more pleasant topics," Piet said, with fake enthusiasm, "So what's your plan? Are you sure you want to take a chance in a dead city? The authorities frown on citizens exploring them. You could be arrested. And there are other dangers such as feral animals."

"Oh, I should be okay," Colt grinned. "These citizens are going to take me up along the coast, and I'll sneak in from the beach."

"Will you go in at dawn?" Piet looked at the water rats.

"That would mean going on the water at night, and I'm not doing that for any amount of old money nor cash tokens," Old Matley growled. The female glanced up, alarmed, then resumed staring at her hands.

"I've heard about water monsters," Arlo said carefully.

"It's not the water monsters. It's the bergs, big piles of crap that the old people dumped in the water before the plague. It clumped together and floats around. Out away from shore there are bergs the size of villages and they don't move much, but in close the smaller ones move around. If you're out in a small boat at night, you can run into one before you know it and once you're in the water, you're dead."

"The water's that toxic?" Piet asked.

"Yep." He glanced at his companion then at Colt.

"We better get goin'." He drained his glass of green liquor.

They all stood and fist bumped once again.

Ana had finally convinced Jordi to get away from the cottage before Bruxton returned. She had planned to snoop around the neighborhood while he was gone and her plans had been interrupted by Jordi's appearance. She was having trouble processing his news about Oren and Linnet. She had known Jordi for years, both at university and when the two couples had shared the flat. This Jordi was nothing like the citizen she had thought she knew. That Jordi would have been incapable of killing anyone, especially religionists. She tried to remember any conversations they had ever had about religionists and nothing special came to mind. She could only infer that his serious injury at the hand of Irene Thorne and having Teegan murdered soon afterward had unhinged him. As a scientist, she rejected the idea as too simplistic. Ironically, Bruxton was purportedly a specialist in mental cases. Too bad she could not discuss this case with him.

Finally she and Jordi decided that he would hide in the shed in the yard behind the cottage until night fell, then summon the aircar and take it into the countryside, all the while trying to raise Colt on the comm. He would return to the cottage the next day after Bruxton had left and help Ana explore the dead city. She hated letting him keep the comm and regretted it even more when Bruxton arrived, earlier than expected and obviously excited.

"It's time for you to come with me," he said, when he entered the cottage.

"Why?"

"He's here. The Sojourner is here. He wants to see you."

"What for?"

"I don't know. He's very excited," the fat healer bounced eagerly, pulling at her arm.

"You'll have to give me a minute," Ana said, glancing at the toilet.

"Hurry. I'll wait in the aircar." He floated out to the vehicle.

In the cottage, Ana recovered the pistol and bullets, stuffing them in her backpack without taking time to reload.

There was nothing to do but go with him, hoping Jordi was watching from the shed and would be able to follow her.

29

Colt was freezing cold in the little open boat and sick of the water rat's chatter. They had left the dock and headed away from the coast toward open water. The sky brightened as they moved away from land and dodged among a few small floating bergs, some of them crowned with plants. Old Matley said the waters around large bergs farther away from shore were the best spots for fishing. Some were used by the Conclave for water purification facilities and fish processing plants.

No monsters swam up from the murky depths.

Colt kept an eye peeled for the Conclave's spy satellites. He interrupted another third-hand story about giant leviathans leaping into the sky to destroy ships to ask Old Matley about the satellites. The water rat said he never saw any over the water. But, he added, there wasn't much for the satellites to see. The area was remote from commercial shipping lanes, used only by fishing boats. Once in a while there would be a report of a ship in the area flying the

Conclave's ensign, possibly going to service one of the installations on the big bergs away from shore.

He couldn't say whether there were surveillance satellites over the dead city at present; he hadn't been there in a couple of years. In his youth, there were very few.

"You gotta remember, in them days citizens was scared to death of things in the dead city; the paper virus would kill you, and there was a lot of books and stuff left. And those old folks had little animals living with them. They all carried the plague. When citizens died or were evacuated they were left behind. So citizens were afraid. Of course, we was kids so we thought nothing would happen to us. And nothing did, much, except a buddy of mine fell and broke his leg in two places. That was pretty funny."

They had agreed that Old Matley would kill the engine on the little boat and row Colt under the abandoned amusement pier from which he could easily climb up to street level. It was clear once they arrived that this point of access was still in use. Recently discarded garbage was strewn about and a couple of newish, sturdy-looking crates were tucked carefully above the water line.

Colt fist bumped the water rat and made arrangements to be picked up in three days.

The Amusement Park label on Arlo's silk map had meant nothing to Colt. The Conclave's writings frequently pointed out that the old people, pre-plague, had been excessively hedonistic and self-involved. The park dedicated to amusement seemed to epitomize all the failings of the ancestors. Although now faded and crumbling, the signs outlined in lights, the extravagantly colored horses, the huge wheels meant obviously to spin epitomized colorful gaiety and exuberance. Towering over the park was a huge, skeletal wheel, still pretty sturdy, easy for someone with Colt's skills to climb to the top.

He had been keeping an eye on the sky, regardless of Old Matley's assurances that surveillance satellites were not in use, and had seen nothing. Tucking his heavy backpack securely behind a pile of debris, Colt commenced to work his way to the top of the wheel. None of the buildings in the dead city, at least those near the shore, were more than a couple of stories and the huge wheel towered over them. From his vantage point, he could see the city laid out much like Arlo's map had depicted it. This city did not have the lowering pall common for populated areas under the New Dispensation and he could see quite a long way.

The amusement park pier had been central to the commercial area. Opposite the park was the main square and broad streets radiated outward, intersecting smaller squares. Two of the five major streets petered out among smaller streets. Two of the boulevards terminated in the areas that had been labeled Refinery and Laboratory on the map. Each consisted of a good-sized cluster of buildings. Beyond the refinery, which was farthest from the waterfront, was an immense collection of undulating greenish pools that Colt took to be the algae farms used for producing fuel. Each facility had a large central building with numerous outbuildings. The main building on his left, the laboratory, was several stories high.

More to the point, in a large plaza fronting the facilities, Colt could see many aircars and small moving dots that were indisputably citizens. Lots and lots of them.

After surveying the dead city, he finally concluded that activity was confined to the far edge near the laboratory and generating plant. Neither aircars nor pedestrians could be seen in the areas near the waterfront.

Satisfied, he began to climb down the huge wheel where some of the seats still swung from rusting axels. He enjoyed imagining the huge wheel spinning and wondered how fast it could go. He saw, as he worked his way down the escarpment, that the superstructure was covered with lights. Bright lights, he imagined. Just the kind of frivolity the New Dispensation had risen above.

Recovering his backpack, Colt began to work his way down the boulevard that lead to the laboratory. If Ana were anywhere, and he refused to believe she was not still alive, she would be in a laboratory.

Jordi had just settled in for an uncomfortable nap when he heard an aircar door open and saw Bruxton hurry into the cottage. His early return was suspicious. Watching him bustle toward the door, Jordi could see he was excited about something. He was doubly sure when Bruxton appeared a few minutes later and activated the aircar.

Before Jordi could decide what to do, Ana emerged from the cottage with her backpack. Jordi saw her glance toward the shed before she got into the aircar and it whooshed off.

Hurrying inside, Jordi found a hurriedly written note from Ana saying simply, "we went to the lab."

He had no idea where that was.

After putting in a brief appearance at the aircar races, chatting with a couple of bystanders to reinforce their presence, Piet and Arlo moseyed along the shoreline to Rick's villa. The door to the outer gate was closed and locked. "I don't know why he bothers," Piet said, "There's an external staircase to the roof with a gate a child could jump.

They continued ringing the bell and after several minutes, the peephole opened.

"Oh, it's you," Rick ungraciously opened the door, looking at the two of them. "Where's Colt?"

"He went to the dead city," Arlo said.

"Fool." Rick relocked the door carefully after them.

"He's looking for Ana," Piet said.

Following Rick across the courtyard, he continued, "We saw Colt in Deep Cove. He told us about Jordi."

Rick unlocked the door to the main part of the villa and when they had passed through, relocked it also.

"C'mon upstairs," Rick said. "I need a drink."

In the filthy kitchen, Rick grabbed a bottle of cognac and three smudged glasses.

"Ilsa's in her room," Rick poured a healthy belt of the cognac into one of the dirty glasses and drank it in one gulp. "I'll tell her you're here."

Piet and Arlo looked at each other without speaking. Rick's behavior was unprecedented. He rarely drank, and then only a glass of fine wine. Moreover, his hair was uncombed, hanging around his face, rather than pulled back in its customary neat bun.

While Rick was out of the room, Arlo took the

three glasses into the kitchen and returned with three clean ones.

As they waited, Piet poured himself a small drink, which he did not want, and strolled over to the edge of the terrace that overlooked the coastline. The dead city was not visible from this spot, but he knew it was not that far away. Immediately below' Rick's villa the beach gave way to a rocky coastline backed up by a heavily treed woodland that stretched into the distance.

"I wonder if one could work their way through the woods and reach the dead city. Surveillance satellites could not penetrate the trees." Piet said.

Arlo joined him. "There are probably wild animals in there," he said.

"As long as there are no wild people. We'll ask Rick."

"If we can get a straight answer out of him. He's drunk." Arlo said. "He used to get like this in the old days, at university, before he fell for Ilsa."

"She's a beautiful woman," Piet mused.

"She wants to be taken care of," Arlo's voice was disapproving.

"Some citizens are like that."

"Yeah, but what happens when the other person needs to be taken care of, like Rick." Arlo said despondently. "He's a wreck."

When they turned to go back to their seats, Rick had reappeared and was sitting with his hands on his knees, unsteadily holding another glass of cognac.

"Ilsa sends her regards, but she is unable to entertain visitors," he said, in a surprisingly sober voice.

Then he started to cry.

The two other citizens looked at each other and, as one, put their glasses down, preparing to take their leave.

Rick was blubbering. "Ilsa led him on, the poor idiot. His life was falling apart. He lost Teegan, who buffered him. He loved her even though she screwed around with everyone. Ana was kidnapped. Kidnapped! Crazy people came in helicopters and shot him. Then Ilsa worked on him. She wanted Oren dead, not Linnet, who did all the work around here, but Oren. She was terrified of Oren.

"Oh, she's good at it. She did it to me, back at the university. She was so beautiful and vulnerable. And her voice is sublime." He took a deep drink of cognac and blew his nose on his shirttail.

"She hated performing in front of strangers, hated traveling to other cities to perform. She had been brought up in a crèche for talented children, and they wanted her to repay them by performing. They brought pressure on her.

"Then she was tested and found to be fertile. She became completely distraught. I thought she was going to suicide. I had to do something, so I gave up my position as a professor and brought her here."

"And we were fine until the world intruded."

Guilty, because he had been part of the world that had intruded on Rick's refuge, Piet looked at his glass; he had drunk more than he intended.

"I hate the New Dispensation, the world ruled by the Conclave of Elders. I read, you know," he gave them a challenging look, "I have books from the past. There are lots of them in the dead city. Before the plague, citizens were free, free to express themselves, free to be religionists, if they wanted to. Then the plague came and the group that became the Conclave of Elders took full advantage of the chaos."

"It wasn't better," Arlo protested. "There were wars everywhere, famine, disease. The planet was dying, the oceans were full of garbage."

Rick wasn't listening. Much like, Piet thought, what he had heard about the old people. They constantly fought with one another.

Rick glared at Arlo. "If there is an afterlife, like the religionists say, your ancestor has much to answer for."

Arlo, who had returned to staring moodily into his glass, waiting for a good moment to leave, suddenly glanced upward, fully alert.

Piet was startled also. Looking at him, Rick said, "Oh, you didn't know. Your buddy Arlo Gauss is the descendant of Johannes Zapf-Gauss, the architect of the New Dispensation."

"I don't know what you are talking about," Piet snapped.

"No. It's part of history. And history's not part of the curriculum in schools under the New Dispensation. They don't teach it, or at least, only as approved by the Conclave. They say they want citizens to look to the future, not the past, which was full of errors and unsanctioned thinking. But all the ideas for the New Dispensation came from a paper written by Arlo's ancestor."

"Not all," Arlo said, sadly.

"No?" challenged Rick.

"No. He outlined how a one-world government could arise following a natural disaster, how a well-placed organization with the right principles could take charge, what it should stand for. He never advocated loosing a plague or any other kind of devastation."

"You think the plague was loosed?" Piet asked, surprised at hearing that word come out of his mouth but more interested than surprised at the idea. It had always been widely mooted; always outside the hearing of the Conclave, of course.

"Don't you?" Arlo asked. "It was just too convenient."

"What did your ancestor think?" Rick asked nastily.

"He didn't know about the New Dispensation. He died from the plague. He was one of the first victims. My father was very proud of him. He told me all about him."

"Did he tell you where he lived?" Rick smirked.

"Not that it matters," Arlo said indifferently.

"He lived in the dead city. Just up the coast from here. He retired here to do his writing, to design the New Dispensation."

"I didn't know that," Arlo said. Thinking about his ancestor left him sad. The New Dispensation did not encourage attachments to ancestors. In fact, they insisted on referring to the people who had gone before as the "old people." Under the New Dispensation, each citizen was a new citizen.

He had a sudden urge to seek out his ancestor's old home. He remembered his father remarking, "I think you are very similar in character to the old citizen." And Arlo would become angry because he didn't want to be similar to an old citizen. He had wanted to be a new citizen.

Piet stood up, suddenly tired of the conversation and the company, needing to walk off some of the cognac.

"Please give our condolences to Ilsa. If we can be of assistance in any way, please call on us. We are staying in the village for a few days."

Rick remained seated, waving his fist at them to be bumped. They ignored him.

As they strolled back to the village, Piet said, "I was surprised at the harshness of your comments about the old people. I thought you were working against the Conclave, to return conditions to the way they were in the old days. The freedoms that Rick spoke about."

"Yeah, I know," Arlo responded. "But in the last few years, I have been rethinking my views. My teachers at university, especially Professor Tillman, were charismatic citizens, very persuasive, especially to young people who are impatient with the structure imposed by the C.E. As a student in the Marketing and Propaganda Department, I learned how to manipulate citizens and in the process I realized how, under the New Dispensation, we were manipulated. They were trying to break down structures and mental constructs that had been in place for eons. In fact, some of the professors claimed things like family bonds were innate and couldn't be altered. Some even said that war was inevitable and should be embraced for strengthening the citizenry. They were full of intriguing ideas.

They were especially convinced that religionism could not be eradicated. They argued that our species was so mentally weak that it would always need religionist explanations for things it didn't understand; we should go back to the old ways when citizens could be religious if they wanted. Some advocated slowly introducing the New Dispensation as a religion. In fact, my department had several brilliant citizens working on ways to do that. At the time, I thought that was the ultimate betrayal of the trust the citizens had in the Conclave, too cynical, too duplicitous.

"Then I met your uncle and he introduced me to the beliefs of the Osirans and they made a lot of sense to me. The idea that the deity had somehow become lost behind a barrier of unbelief, that we could bring the great one back to us and the world would be perfect. It seemed to avoid all the bad elements of most belief systems but provided an explanation for why things were screwed up. And it provided hope.

"Then it struck me. I was as mentally weak as the religionists we learned about at university. I wasn't a new citizen; I was an old person, like those who had practically destroyed the world. Then I began to think that destroying the Conclave was a bad idea; that the ideas of the New Dispensation might be better for citizens, for the world."

Arlo sighed and shook his head. "I just don't know the answer, Piet."

"No . . ." was all Piet could find to say.

Arlo looked at Piet. He still resembled the young citizen Piet remembered. The kid who had been fascinated with the Subs when many of the upside citizens considered them a myth. The kid who had sought him out despite warnings and imagined dangers. And the kid who followed charismatic teachers and killed his fellow citizens in pursuit of his ideal.

"What do you think, Piet?"

"As I always tell Beau, I try not to think."

Arlo could not let it go. "Do you think our species is despicable?"

"Our species? No."

Before Arlo could say anything more, Piet held up his hand for silence and hurried on into Deep Cove with Arlo trailing behind.

No more words were exchanged on the return trip. The village was still awash in the race crowds so Piet returned to their rental for relief from the noise. He missed the solitude of his home in the Subs.

Arlo decided to wander over to the bar and see if he could find the water rat who had taken Colt to the dead city. No comm frequencies were functioning; the bar was loud with the complaints of restive race crowds who could not reach their bookies.

30

In the dead city, Bruxton's aircar touched down in a large parking lot and immediately plugged itself into a charger. Numerous other aircars, some of them quite expensive, were parked outside a complex of buildings. Although obviously old, pre-plague, the buildings had the unmistakable look of all labs, expanses of white marble, huge windows, and miles of mysterious silver tubes. The ensign of the Conclave flew above the highest building.

As they approached the door, a smiling citizen in a white coat ran toward them.

"Citizen Bruxton, you're here," he caroled, fist bumping Bruxton.

Ana immediately labeled him an idiot.

"The Sojourner is anxious to meet with Dr. Bede." The greeter's mouth continued smiling as he turned to Ana—his eyes were less friendly. Like Bruxton, he had a strand of amber worry beads around his wrist.

"Yes, of course." Bruxton held the door for Ana, as they followed their grinning greeter into a rotunda topped by a glass dome. Everything was immaculate and expensive. Once inside, he turned to them, the smile gone, and said, "the Sojourner wants to meet with Dr. Bede in his private chamber. Alone."

Bruxton looked disappointed, then, strangely, took Ana's hand and kissed it before ambling through a nearby doorway.

"This way," the greeter led Ana into a modern elevator, activating it with a keycard. He remained silent through the trip to the top floor where the door opened into what was obviously an anteroom, empty except for an antique settee and a round mirror that was almost certainly a surveillance device.

He pointed at the settee, bowed to the mirror, and stepped back into elevator.

When the door had closed and the indicator showed movement, the door opened and the Sojourner walked through.

"Oh, I see," she said. "Hello, Chandler."

"You don't seem surprised." He removed the heavy robe and mask. He was just as she remembered him, handsome and self-assured.

"I recognized your walk," she said.

He led her down a long hall way and through the door to a beautifully furnished living room.

"This was my grandfather's suite of rooms. He was a director of this laboratory for many years before he became a founder of the Conclave."

"Would you like some food or a glass of wine," he continued. "I don't know how well Bruxton has been taking care of you. For a sanctioned healer, he's something of an idiot."

"I'm fine," Ana said. "He was quite considerate.

He did strangle Teegan. At your direction, he said."

"Oh, well, she's better off now."

He led her into the spacious room and directed her to take a seat. He sat in a chair opposite her.

"I've been looking for Elvistine," he said. "And strangely I haven't been able to find him, even with all the resources of the Conclave." He gave her an interrogative look.

Ana said nothing.

"I was there, you recall, when you told that incredible story about him opening a portal and vanishing."

"What do you want, Chandler?"

"I want your assistance, Ana."

"With what? Opening another portal?" Ana smiled.

"Oh, no. I don't care about your portal, which, by the way, I don't believe is a portal. No, I want your help rebuilding a moon-buster."

Ana was startled.

"Elvistine and Tillman destroyed the plans for that weapon. They decided it was too dangerous."

"I know. But we found an unexploded one and we were able to dismantle it and prepare schematics for the hardware."

"But you couldn't figure out the how the fusion energy triggered the device."

"No. We couldn't do that. But I think you can, Ana."

"What do you want it for? Who's "we"? And what's all this Sojourner business? Isn't that religionist?"

Chandler smiled and jumped to his feet. "I'll tell you all about that over dinner. But first, I want to take you on a tour of the facility. We're very up-to-date here." He glanced at her backpack. "You can leave that here."

"I might want to make some notes," Ana said.

"You can do that later." He led her to a door other than the one they entered. It too opened onto an elevator.

Noting her puzzled look, he said, "This is Chandler's elevator. The other one is strictly for the Sojourner."

Arlo had not spoken with his parents in years. Because of his parents' social standing, they had been able to avoid placing him in a crèche as an infant, had kept him at home, and taken charge of his education. As a child and young citizen, he had always excelled in school and he had embraced the tenets of the New Dispensation. These downplayed the importance of family ties since among the old people, those living before the plague, family ties had led to tribalism then nationalism which in turn fed the old people's commitment to violence and destruction.

For their part, and while never criticizing the Conclave in so many words, his parents had felt the elders had had gone too far in their attempts to disrupt the foundational ties. The adolescent Arlo had despised his parents for these sentiments.

Their relationship had always been problematic. He had always experienced his parents' concern for him as intrusive. They were sanctioned, professional psychohabilitators. From his earliest childhood he had resisted their probing, their insights. They always wanted to know what he was thinking and, worse, feeling. Arlo still felt defensive before the memories of their deep, loving desire to understand him, to help him be a good citizen. Once he went to university, he cut all ties with his family, and he was justified in doing so, as a child of the New Dispensation.

When he had heard, by accident, about his mother's death, the tsunami of emotion nearly undid him. He had felt abandoned in the world. First he had wrestled with the urge to contact his father, then wrestled with the guilt when he didn't.

Now, being reminded of his ancestor, whom he in some way resembled, whether in character or perhaps temperament, he regretted his actions, his disdain. Once more, unwelcome emotions were overcoming him.

As he sat at the bar in Deep Cove, wrestling with feelings he would like to ignore, behind him he heard the fellow, Old Matley, Colt's water rat, talking to his silent companion.

"That city lad paid me good. He should be all right. Ex-military, I bet. Got a gun, knife, who knows what in that backpack. It was heavy. I could tell. So I'll go back and wait for him. Maybe he'll come, maybe he won't. Either way you and me will go to the city for a good time. Lots of citizens heading to the dead city." Arlo heard smacking noises as the gent drank some of his green swill.

Sliding off his stool, Arlo took a seat at their table. He held out his fist but Old Matley just looked angry.

"I heard you talking about my friend Colt. I know he was going to the dead city, but, I'm curious, who are all these other citizens who are heading to the dead city?"

There was an interval while the water rat pondered the question. He glanced at his companion, who just kept staring at her hands while she drank steadily.

Finally, probably unable to think up likely lies, he said, "Don't know. And that's a fact. Just heard stories. Some folks up the coast, by the algae ponds, said there has been lots of traffic, mostly aircars but a few helicopters. That means Conclave. I couldn't guarantee the helicopters. Them citizens is terrible liars."

"Any military?"

"Not that they mentioned." Unable to get any more out of him, Arlo sent over another carafe of whatever it was they were drinking and went to find Piet.

Chandler began his tour with a visit to the algae ponds that extended many klicks into the countryside.

"These algae were introduced by Irene Thorne's father before the New Dispensation. The old people had mostly depleted the planet's natural resources so they had begun looking for other ways to generate the truly incredible quantity of fuel they needed. Irene's grandfather had been working on developing fuel from algae, and her dad, who was a brilliant biologist as well as a savvy businessman, made it happen. Then when the plague reduced the population and the need fell for huge amounts of fuel, these ponds were abandoned. Fortunately the algae didn't completely die. It went dormant or possibly survived by cannibalizing itself. Anyway, it was easy to grow more just by feeding it. So we can now generate the fusion power necessary to recreate and power the moon-buster."

Ana looked around her as the aircar skimmed over

the slightly undulating surface of the ponds. This quantity of algae would create far more fuel than was necessary for creating and powering the weapon.

"I'm only vaguely familiar with the process of turning these organisms into fuel," she lied, then added, truthfully, "It's not my field."

"It's basically a fermentation process," Chandler said authoritatively. Which was really not true. She needed to remember that Chandler was not a scientist; when he said "we" he was including himself with the scientists and engineers whom he controlled.

They took a brief tour of the refinery and generating plant where once again Ana pled ignorance but privately noted that a lot of fuel was being produced.

Chandler then conducted a brief tour of the lab building, showing her the space set aside for the moon-buster project. The other sections, he said, were used for ongoing research to simplify the generation process and improve the algae.

Ana was troubled by the vast quantities of algae that were being grown. It would have been an excessive amount even when the generating plant was producing power for the entire dead city. Now it was excessive for the huge quantities of fuel they were refining. Maybe they were using expensive resources to overproduce algae without a plan in mind. Maybe they just doing it because they didn't know any better. Ana like to think citizens, especially those embedded in the Conclave, were smarter than that.

The algae could be used for things other than converting to fuel. For example, it could be used as a culturing medium for bioengineered organisms, like the plague. Supposedly the plague was created to control invasive species then got out of hand.

She looked at Chandler, horrified. Could he be culturing plague organisms? For what purpose?

31

Piet stood on the back porch of the little shack they rented from the bartender and looked moodily across the water. In the distance he could hear crowd noise from the festival. There were too many people for Piet's taste, pressing in too close. He looked forward to getting to the dead city and was anxious because they had not heard from Colt.

He had been able to get Yonatan on the comm and be assured that Beau was doing as well as could be expected. The boy was still in an induced coma, and Yonatan was staying with him night and day.

Sparrow had disquieting news about the city. The lockdown had been lifted, passage in and out of the city was as open as it had ever been, meaning you still needed passes to get through the gates. But, the brothel keeper had said, the Conclave's military were pouring into the city, taking over the space formerly occupied by the protestors. The protestors, in turn, were being encouraged to return to their home cities leading to sporadic clashes between them and the military.

On a happier note, the House of Blue Leaves was busier than ever and Sparrow had even had to reactivate some retirees. He wasn't too happy, then, when Piet asked him to send one of his kids over to the clinic to personally check on Beau. "Someone reliable," Piet had said, leading to a huffy response from Sparrow that all his staff were reliable. "Someone with good judgment, then," Piet had said and Sparrow said he would do what he could. "Anyway, some of the boys need time to recoup," he said.

Piet was afraid Yonatan was falling in love with Beau, and he didn't really know how Beau would respond. Sparrow had comped Beau services a few times, which Beau had enjoyed, but Piet had not asked for details. Despite their efforts to demystify sex, the New Dispensation had not been able to overcome certain natural affinities, and dis-affinities.

He grinned to himself. The Conclave issued directives that were designed to downplay the importance of personal attractiveness, too, but he knew citizen Sparrow was quite picky about the physical attributes of his employees. No ugly kids in his House.

His good humor was short lived. Yonatan Belasco was a good citizen, a caring healer. Piet had been impressed by his unwillingness to use the suicide devices Piet now carried in his backpack. Devices he would happily use to dispatch the Sojourner citizen when he found him.

Thinking about losing Beau to death was almost more than Piet could bear. If he went with Yonatan, their partnership would be broken up, but he would not grieve. Beau would not stay in the Subs, take over as chief of Grupo Uno as they had planned. Still he would be taken care of, maybe enjoy some happiness. Piet began to think about his happiness with Beau's mother, and his promises to her. Overcome by anguish, he forced himself to find something to take his mind off how much he missed her. He needed something to get mad about.

Arlo's remarks about the Osiran beliefs, which Piet had believed they shared, were disappointing and troubling. A citizen such as Arlo, who took his beliefs seriously and was willing to act on them, could be dangerous, untrustworthy.

Piet had understood how Arlo had felt about the Conclave, back when Arlo was at university and would seek out his friends in the Subs, when Piet's uncle was alive. They had encouraged Arlo to do what he needed to do; that one doesn't always do the safe thing. When Arlo became an Osiran, he said he had put his bomb-throwing past behind him. A certain honesty was expected among the believers.

Dwellers in the Subs were not disloyal to the Conclave. If anything, they were indifferent to its directives. They were not affected by most of the restrictions. They had their own schools, their own clinics. They had brothels and gaming establishments where daring citizens could enjoy the thrill of going to the Subs to party and play.

Most ordinary people upside regarded the Subs as a myth. The authorities supported that illusion because they didn't want to give legitimacy to the area, didn't want citizens going where policing would be difficult. They had a mutually satisfactory, if distant, relationship with Piet, as chief of Grupo Uno.

Rather than bumbling around on their own, they could come to Piet when the situation was sufficiently grave. For most day-to-day crime, Piet was the authority.

While many residents of the Subs had never been upside, Piet, himself, had attended university in another city and traveled extensively. His uncle, the previous chief, thought broad experience of the world was necessary for a leader. Piet had intended for Beau to follow his example.

Grupo Uno always had a policy of ignoring religionists, downplaying any threat. He and Arlo had pooh-poohed Ilsa's concerns about Oren bringing danger on her house. Egging Jordi on to kill him had not solved her problem, either, because if Linnet were found to have been pregnant, the authorities would take a very keen interest in what was going on in the villa. The citizens of the small village likely knew about the incident with Irene Thorne, the presence of a helicopter, the shootings.

Mentally exhausted and agitated, Piet decided it was time to do something, to act. He turned from the porch just as Arlo arrived back at the shack.

Arlo pushed the front door too hard and it made a loud bang. His hands were fisted.

"We have to go to the dead city, now," he said. "Something is going on there. I can feel it."

Piet said nothing and began to throw items into his backpack.

Time to move.

Before they left, Piet made a couple of calls.

Jordi was furious when he found Ana's note, enraged that she had not been more specific. Couldn't she have drawn a map? Something with directions. He tore the little cottage apart looking for a map, an address. He found nothing useful, some clothes, cooking equipment. If there had been a charging station for the aircar he could have plugged his into it and perhaps found out where they went.

He summoned the aircar, heedless of whoever might be watching. He found cold ramen in the kitchen and crammed some in his mouth. He couldn't remember eating and discovered he was starving. With no direction in mind, he retraced his route along the shore toward the downtown area. The most prominent feature was a dock with a huge wheel that stood several stories high. The aircar would not be able to propel itself high enough, but he thought he could possibly climb the wheel and get a view of the dead city.

32

Colt left the amusement park and worked his way toward the laboratory building, keeping out of sight. In the commercial district, most of the sidewalks were covered, relieving him of worry about surveillance satellites. The streets were lined with little shops and cafes. Many of the second floor businesses were cafes with outdoor dining where customers could drink and dine while watching the activity on the streets. Besides startling a few feral cats, he saw no one until the street opened onto a final plaza flanked by one of the lab buildings and a large hotel. The time was getting toward evening and citizens in white lab coats were drifting across the plaza toward the hotel. Someone had ineptly painted a sign on the front of the building which read "Pension: Open All Nite." Colt wondered if just having a lab coat would allow him to blend in or if the staff all knew each other.

He worked his way through an alley to the back of the building, looking for another entrance. A large portion of the ground floor of the hotel was a cafeteria. Once he was in the alley, he could smell food cooking and hear clinking dishes and other sounds. The back end of the building had a couple of open doors and the usual garbage cans. An old-fashioned fire escape led upward.

Unexpectedly a voice said, "Hey, buddy. You new here. Go around to the front and check in."

Colt sketched a salute and hurried around the other side of the hotel where he found a large parking lot with a few aircars scattered near the hotel. Having got a better look at the lab buildings, he could see that they flew the Conclave ensign and a helicopter was parked on the roof of the largest structure.

As far as Colt knew, helicopters were only used by Conclave members on Conclave business.

He strolled among the vehicles, looking for a comfortable spot to hunker down until darkness fell. None of the operators seemed concerned about theft, the vehicles were mostly unlocked and, he assumed, unalarmed. Finally picking a luxurious craft sitting a little higher than the others, he crawled in.

Although the biggest of the nearby aircars, this one was full of crap—bags, boxes, old food, old clothes. And here Colt got lucky because a crumpled white lab coat was discarded on the seat. In the failing light, Colt slipped it on. The key to the aircar was in the pocket.

Placing himself so he could see the hotel and lab, he took a few minutes to doze, knowing motion in his field of vision would awaken him, a handy talent he developed in the military.

When he awoke sometime later, night had closed in. Many of the rooms in the hotel were lighted and citizens could be seen in the cafeteria. Light from the hotel illuminated part of the parking lot but the area around the lab buildings was in shadow except for security lights at several doors. But for a few dim glows, which Colt took to be from lab apparatus, the lab building windows were dark except for several bright oblongs on the top floor.

Colt found himself interested in these windows, which indicated a large laboratory with projects so important they needed attention through the evening. Alternatively there could be an office, some Conclave minion grinding away at paperwork, or possibly a flat for a personage too important to live at the pension.

As he was considering his options, a door opened in the pension and a citizen in waiter garb pushed a trolley encumbered by a long white tablecloth and accouterments for dinner, covered dishes, wine urns, etc. The citizen slowly pushed the trolley across the parking lot, where it was jostled, making noise, and allowing Colt to stroll up behind him.

"Good," Colt said. "I left my key inside."

The citizen did not look at him. "You guys would lose your asses if they weren't glued on," he muttered, continuing to push the trolley toward a door, which he opened with a key card, thus answering one of Colt's questions.

The door opened on a small service area with a beat up elevator and a swinging door apparently leading to the main part of the building. Colt continued through the swinging door into a long hallway. Stopping just inside, he watched the waiter summon the elevator without needing a keycard and maneuver the trolley into the elevator, swearing as the tablecloth caught on the door. Colt watched the floor indicators until they stopped at "Pent." A penthouse, he thought, not an office.

The indicator stayed on "Pent" so long he was beginning to wonder whether the waiter was going to serve through the entire dinner when the elevator chimed and the floor indicators began to decrease. At the bottom, the door opened and the waiter, without the trolley, hurried through the little room and out the door leaving Colt a few seconds to barge out of the hallway and stop the elevator's doors closing.

As the doors closed, Colt checked his weapons and wished the elevator doors had peepholes. The car had doors opening at both ends; one labeled "Labs" and one labeled "Private." Colt pushed the "P" button and the car ascended slowly and noisily. Once at the top, the doors stayed closed. Opening the "Labs" door led to a long dark corridor. Uncarpeted and spare, it looked like another of the many facilities where Colt had visited Ana through the years.

After waiting a few seconds, the doors closed. Taking a deep breath, Colt pushed the door labeled "Private." The door opened and Colt stepped into a small, lighted prep kitchen. Hot water bubbled softly next to a waiting samovar and a tray with two tea glasses. A cold wine urn held a full, open bottle of white wine, and, mercifully, the swinging door possessed a small window.

The door opened on a small, elegant dining room. Ana and Chandler Besdine were seated on opposite sides of a beautiful pre-plague antique table, the top shimmering with china and glassware. Colt's entire being lit up when he saw Ana, alive and unharmed.

She was too thin and tired, but also weighed down with some indefinable concern that went beyond exhaustion. He had seen Ana and Elvistine work themselves to the limits of endurance in pursuit of Elvistine's cockamamie idea that mental exhaustion increased creativity by breaking down conventional thought patterns. Whatever Ana was suffering went beyond that.

Chandler merely looked like Chandler—handsome, relaxed, unreadable.

Colt took a moment to stick a wadded up napkin in the elevator door so a returning waiter could not call it downstairs then gently cracked open the swinging door into the dining room enough to hear the conversation.

Ana was saying, "What exactly are you going to do with the moon-buster?"

Chandler laughed and poured some wine in her glass. "I'll tell you that if you tell me what exactly happened to Elvistine."

Ana did know what happened to Elvistine, but she wasn't sure she wanted to tell Chandler. She said, "You know Elvistine had begun working on controlling time because he was aging, facing death. He had a congenital heart anomaly that was killing him. He felt he owed it to the elders to stay alive, to further their wonderful plan, and repay them for their support.

"In the process of researching time, we concluded there are an infinite number of dimensions or realities or timelines, call them what you will, parallel to ours and they are all our reality but with slightly different event horizons and on slightly different timelines. The only one we could actually view through the portal was quite similar to our own. We theorized that the farther you go through parallel realities the more dissimilar they become. But we are not able to penetrate beyond the closest one.

"The veil between the dimensions is extremely thin—but unbridgeable by ordinary means. Citizens whisper that beings like angels and things like UFOs are from other dimensions that have somehow jumped through the veil, but I don't believe that."

"What are they then," Chandler asked, intrigued.

"Citizens can convince themselves of anything if the need is great enough. I think they are mental constructions that have taken on some level of substantial reality."

"Yes, I could use that," Chandler mused.

Ana was puzzled by his remark but continued, "When Elvistine started fooling around with the formulae governing time and applying some of the little-known byproducts from our generation of fusion energy to pry at the veil, he started something he could not control. He tore a hole in the veil.

"Interestingly, while we couldn't go forward into the future in our own reality, we could do so in the parallel reality. Elvistine keep going farther and farther into the future. He was curious about the future, about future discoveries in science. But then he went so far into the future, beyond the termination of the reality to . . . ." She paused. Chandler stopped in the process of raising a wine glass to his lips. Colt realized he had stopped breathing.

"To nothing. Literally." She looked at Chandler with an expression of despair.

"Ridiculous," Chandler snapped.

Ana shook her head sadly.

"The portal is literally the unrealized potentiality that existed before the triggering event that gave birth to the multiple realities. Apparently all realities will eventually wind down and die."

"Fascinating, but irrelevant," Chandler said. "So the portal opens onto primordial chaos or whatever."

Chandler himself paused, struck by a thought. "You're not telling me that Elvistine found a way to physically cross the veil, as you called it, between realities."

"No. When Elvistine realized what he had done by creating the portal, he gave in to despair. He discovered two things." Ana held up one finger. "He found he could not close the portal. And"—she held up a second finger— "the primordial chaos, as you term it, is draining the energy from our reality. If we don't find a way to stop it, our reality is doomed."

Chandler's face mirrored the astonishment that Colt was feeling as he eavesdropped on the other side of the door.

"That cannot be true," Chandler protested. "It's ridiculous. Nothing cannot exist, by definition it could not get bigger. It must be a black hole."

"Call it what you will. Your flunkies who are monitoring the portal will tell you that, even if nothing is not getting bigger, the world is getting smaller."

"So Elvistine thought that by futzing around with time, he had merely managed to destroy our universe."

"Exactly. That's why he committed suicide."

"Why bother," Chandler said. "If he was dying of heart disease and our universe is being eaten by a hole in time, why not just wait it out?"

Ana wiped her eyes on a napkin. "I loved him, you know, like a father," she said. "He had too much imagination. He felt so guilty. And, for Desmond, the very idea of nothing terrified him; it invaded his dreams. The universe and everything in it . . . space, time . . . would cease to exist. And he had caused it. He felt the least he could do was kill himself."

"Ana, this just can't be true," Chandler said. "Matter cannot be destroyed."

"It isn't being destroyed. It's dying. The bonds that hold everything together are disappearing. It's no different from what happens in a fusion pistol or grenade. When the pistol or grenade is activated, it dissolves the bonds of matter. The person or object affected simply disappears from our view. All that remains is infinitesimal dust. But the fusion pistol simply releases a burst of energy. The portal releases concomitant energy continually."

"Well, I don't believe it." Chandler made a gesture, sat up, moved on. "It doesn't make any difference to my plans. I suppose I don't even care if the universe is being eaten by primordial chaos. As long as I fulfill my promise to my grandfather, I'm going to destroy the Conclave of Elders, the consistory, everything. And you, Ana, are going to help me."

"What will you do if I won't help you?" Ana asked. "Let Bruxton strangle me too?"

"Oh, no, that would be too kind. I'll do something worse. I'll destroy your intellect."

Ana looked shocked. "What?"

"I'll destroy your intellect. The Conclave labs have come up with a number of useful gadgets in their quest for control of unsanctioned thoughts. They are so opposed to simple execution. I honor them for that but it seems shortsighted.

"Now they have come up with an item that acts selectively on the parts of the brain that control intelligence. Unfortunately, it doesn't increase intelligence. When used systematically, it slowly decreases the citizen's intellectual capacity. Very unpleasant for the citizen. And usually not very useful. Most of the unsanctioned convictions citizens hold are not based on intelligence.

"In your case, Ana, it would be a suitable punishment. If you don't help me, I'll return you to the intellectual equal of a four year old. Slowly. And, if you don't believe me, I can show you videos of citizens who were experimental subjects. The high point of their day is playing with blocks."

Ana was too shocked to speak. Before she could process the implications of what Chandler had said, he spoke again, musing, "There is a way out for you, of course."

She just looked at him. He was happy to note that she looked terrified.

"You could tell me where to find Elvistine. He would help me and your conscience would be clear."

Ana shook her head. "I told you. Elvistine suicided. Maybe you can get Tillman out of the stasis chamber. He would probably help you to avoid going back."

Chandler was getting angry.

"Tillman isn't in the stasis chamber. He never was. Tillman is dead. He was old and had a heart attack. The Conclave did what they could for him but it wasn't enough.

"So I guess it's up to you, Ana. We'll start tomorrow."

Chandler stood up, began to gather the dishes. They had had tofu stroganoff, which looked delicious to Colt, who was hungry. He was backing up through the service kitchen to hide in the hallway on the other side of the elevator when Ana spoke.

Chandler had turned toward the swinging door, dishes in both hands. Colt could see his face.

"If your plan is to destroy the Conclave, why are you culturing the plague?" Ana said.

Chandler was shocked, Colt watched his face change; shocked and enraged. Later he wondered why he had not just killed him then.

Chandler turned and backed through the swinging door, placing the plates on the trolley, and without turning around, returned to the dining room. Colt watched his fighting ball swing gently from side to side.

"You figured that out, did you?" he said.

"There's too much algae being grown to provide power for a moon-buster or two. It figured you were going to do something else with it. The plague was just a guess."

"It's important to have more than one arrow in your quiver," he said. "Let's have dessert and we'll talk about it in the morning." He moved out of Colt's line of sight and returned with two small dishes.

Ana had a couple of bites then pushed it away. Chandler ate his with gusto. Contemplating genocide seemed to give him an appetite.

Colt had decided to give it a few minutes, then snoop around the suite. He was confident he would not be caught. He stepped back into the shadows of the elevator as Chandler set the two dishes on the trolley and the lights went off in the dining room. While he waited, he wolfed down Ana's bread pudding, his favorite.

Within a very short time, he vision began to blur and he felt light-headed. The dish had been drugged. Alarmed for himself, but also for Ana, he tried to move but fell to his knees. Unable to do more, he pushed aside the long tablecloth covering the trolley and curled up on the bottom shelf.

Jordi found the big wheel, but he couldn't climb it. Since being wounded his strength was gone. The area around the wheel was puzzling. Giant gaudy pictures of food and weird faces were painted on the buildings and piles of meaningless girders indicated structures whose former use was unclear. He found a puzzling pile of painted horses. He had seen pictures of horses in videos, of course; citizens had ridden them. He tried to imagine why the old people made wooden horses.

Feeling dizzy, he left the enclosure and began hurrying through the streets of the dead city, almost running. To keep a low profile, he abandoned the aircar near the big wheel on the pier, where he could find it again. By going inland, away from the water, he thought he would find citizens and where there were citizens, he would find the healer who had killed Teegan and taken Ana away. He kept checking his weapon, making sure it was handy. He wished Colt were with him. Colt was a citizen you needed in this situation.

He really needed to get some sleep. He was beginning to hallucinate ghosts; they were watching him from doorways and vacant windows. No matter how firmly he told himself they were not real, he could still see them.

And then it struck him. They were real. This was a

dead city, full of the ghosts of the old people who lived here and died from the plague. Old people who made wooden horses and giant wheels. Old people who hated him because he was still alive.

They were stalking him.

33

Neither Piet nor Arlo was happy with the idea of taking a boat to the dead city and they didn't care for Old Matley's demeanor either. Under normal circumstances, Piet would have had no concerns handling a scurvy specimen like the water rat. Proximity to the water made the difference. Large bodies of water . . . frightened wasn't a word he wanted to use . . . troubled him, they were so limitless and hostile. And, if Old Matley could be believed, which, in principle, Piet doubted, the water was dangerous to swim in for more than a brief period of time.

"I'll drop you where I dropped the other guy," Old Matley said, as he pushed off from the dock. "I'm going to stay a little closer to the shore than usual because I want to get back to Deep Cove before dark."

Piet and Arlo huddled together, Arlo watching the shore and Piet watching Old Matley. As they got farther from the coast, they began to see big vague smudges in the distance like mountains rising from the water. Occasionally a light would flash, as if they were occupied. Old Matley explained about the piles of debris dumped by the old people, how the debris had clumped together into berms, they were called. Some were big enough that they no longer floated free and could be used for things like water treatment plants. He had been told that rich citizens who wanted privacy sought out the bigger ones and used them for vacation homes. He had not personally seen one. It was a rumor.

He had explained that fishing was better in the vicinity of the bigger berms. Smaller berms that floated free presented major nighttime dangers to boats.

Late in the day, the light was flat, the sky overcast. As Old Matley talked about the berms, he kept looking nervously toward the horizon. When Arlo asked what he was watching for he shrugged.

"Don't know. I don't like this kind of light."

Arlo didn't like that kind of response. He started envisioning the giant water spiders which figured prominently in conversations at the bar. Giant water spiders were reputed to wrap their legs around boats, even large fishing boats, and drag them under the water. A little open boat such as this one would be child's play to a giant water spider. While less imaginative than Arlo, Piet was happy to reach the dead city and pull up under the pier. Before he let Old Matley leave, he questioned him closely about the possibility of going overland, on foot, back to Deep Cove.

Old Matley said it was possible if you didn't mind big animals. A few citizens lived in the woods but,

Old Matley said, they wouldn't bother you if you didn't bother them. Piet assured him that was his personal motto.

They had previously agreed that the water rat would return to the spot under the pier periodically for a week, waiting for them. He would be available by comm, too, if they needed him, but he would not, he insisted, come at night.

As Colt had previously, they noticed signs that the area under the pier was frequently used. Piet checked his weapons and Arlo, as was his custom, was unarmed. They easily climbed to street level, avoiding the area with the big wheel, and followed Arlo's map toward the generating refinery where the water rat had reported rumors of activity.

After walking for a while, the silence began to weigh on them. The empty buildings were filled with shadows and the subdued sounds of, they hoped, small animals. The occasional harsh calls of birds startled them, causing them to glance nervously upward.

Finally, to fill the silence, Piet said, "You never told me about your falling out with Tillman."

"I didn't fall out with him. In fact he saved my life." Arlo snapped, then continued more calmly. "At university, I got to know Tillman pretty well. He was my mentor and I thought we had a lot in common; we were both disgusted at the death grip the Conclave had on the planet. He said in the old days, citizens took a lot of responsibility for their own governments. He even claimed the Conclave had engineered the plague to get power.

"Tillman claimed the elders would never

voluntarily give up control and would have to be destroyed by armed force. He said militant cadres were forming, armed cadres, all over the planet. Once the Conclave was destroyed, a group of enlightened citizens would take their place and teach citizens how to once again take control of their government.

"Citizen groups, including the protestors in the camp in the city, were being formed to augment the armed cadres. At the proper time, they too would be armed to support the new government.

"In the meantime guerilla actions were needed to make citizens alert to the repression flowing from the Conclave. Authorities would respond with excessive force to the bombings and citizens would wake up."

"But they didn't," Piet said. "Not right away."

Arlo looked at his friend with tragic eyes.

"I know. The bombing targets were strangely chosen. Sometimes, but not always, selected for maximum effect. They were very specific. I became suspicious. I felt that Tillman and I could make better choices, but he said the targets were selected by the coordinators. I finally concluded they were not intended as guerilla actions at all. They were assassinations."

Arlo paused but Piet said nothing.

"I was sure of it after the final bombing at the elementary school. The target was well chosen but the coordinators directed that the bombing take place during a prize presentation in the gymnasium when the children and the school officials were present."

"Let me guess," Piet said. "The prize was being presented by someone from the C.E."

Arlo nodded.

"He, of course, died along with several hundred

children."

Arlo nodded again.

Piet continued. "And, as I remember the aftermath, the authorities did pay attention. The news focused on the children but I'm guessing they were most outraged because of the death of an elder. They very quickly identified you and Tillman as the perpetrators; Tillman was arrested and sent to a stasis chamber but you escaped."

"We both escaped. Immediately after the bombing, Tillman came to me and said we had been sold out. He had an aircar ready, and we left town. The last time I saw him, he dropped me off at a commune in the mountains and took off. The people in the commune were sympathetic to the movement. I was there for a few weeks when I heard that Tillman had been captured and put into stasis."

"But now you don't think that was true." Piet said.

"No."

"Where is Tillman then?"

Arlo shook his head despondently. "I don't know."

"But killing those children. That was a terrible thing."

"It was, and don't you see, what's worse," Arlo said, "those children's lives didn't mean anything. It doesn't matter whether they lived or died, the citizenry is going extinct. The plague reduced the population below the critical mass needed for survival and the consequent infertility of a high percentage of women means there is no replacement of adequate population. In a few years, the last citizens will die, if not of old age, then of disease and starvation. We may hang on as ragtag tribes for a few years, but eventually we will be gone. The planet will be left to the animals."

Piet couldn't argue with this assessment. He had traveled extensively as part of his education and had noticed the size of cities under the New Dispensation compared with the vast dead cities of the old people. He felt a profound, indefinable grief as he walked through the remains of the once vibrant city. Among the faded gay facades of the seaside town, he imagined he heard laughter and music.

They walked on for a few minutes accompanied only by the shrieks of birds. Usually taciturn, Piet couldn't stand the silence.

"What are you hoping to accomplish in the dead city? Is your only goal to help Colt rescue Ana?"

"I'm hoping to find my ancestor's home, his study, his papers. I want to know if he was truly the architect of the New Dispensation."

"Then what? The truth will set you free?"

"Freedom doesn't exist," Arlo said bitterly.

Piet decided it was time to shut up.

In the city, Yonatan watched over Beau and contemplated a career change. The directive from the Conclave had ordered him to use their inventions to murder his patients in a manner so horrible he hated to think about it. He had always been touched by the despair that drove citizens to suicide. In medical school he had heard stories from older healers of mass suicides after the plague was fully established. Citizens would watch their whole families, their towns, die, and seeing no hope for the future and the death of their collective memory, their past, had killed themselves in droves.

For personages of Yonatan's social and professional standing, disregarding the directives of the Conclave was not an option. He could lose everything, including, if he was unlucky, his freedom.

Meanwhile he watched over Beau, not with sexual interest, as Piet imagined, but with a need he couldn't put into words. It was like the urge that led him to becoming a healer, the urge to care, to heal, to nurture. He was standing in for Piet, taking care of Piet's child like he would take care of his own child.

Chandler watched Ana yawn after she ate the bread pudding. Knowing she would nibble at it, he had added an extra large dose of knock out drops. He needed her asleep rather than snooping around the suite; even without the weapon he had removed from her backpack.

After virtually carrying her to a guest room, knowing she would be asleep in minutes, he entered another guest suite where equipment had been set up for making videos. Donning his sojourner disguise, he summoned the technician who would do the filming and seated himself in an ornate, throne-like chair, assuming a meditative posture.

How convenient that the original sojourner adopted a costume which essentially hid individual features. That citizen's motivations were more spiritual than Chandler's; he had worn the disguise to represent himself not as an individual but as the voice of the Man in the Sky. And Chandler felt a kinship with the original sojourner because he too had been planning to overthrow the Conclave. Although they had shared goals, he had had to modify the original sojourner's plan somewhat. That citizen planned to do something he called passive resistance, something that did not involve violence.

The technician knocked on the door, giving Chandler time to pull the hood over his head. Affixed to the front of the hood was a veil that completely hid the wearer's face. Sewn into the veil was a small microphone that distorted the speaker's voice. The latter device was Chandler's addition to the costume. He was anxious that no one should identify him as the Sojourner, who was going to bring down the Conclave of Elders and end the New Dispensation.

The technician groveled into the room and set up the equipment, then sat in worshipful silence while the Sojourner delivered his homily. As he spoke, Chandler silently gave thanks that the now deceased former Sojourner had left behind a library of videos outlining his conversion to belief in the Man in the Sky and the messages and directives he had received from that mythical personage. As Chandler parroted them, modified to downplay the former passive message and stress the need for violence against the Conclave, he felt a rush of power. Initially he had felt revulsion at the message, at the deluded followers, and, strangely, at himself for participating in the vicious charade. His grandfather had been one of the strongest opponents of religionism. Then, as he had become comfortable in the Sojourner's habit, he had begun to enjoy the feeling of command. He had realized there were multitudes of followers huddled in cells throughout the world, waiting for his words. Through his contacts at the Citadel, as the Conclave's headquarters were known, he had learned that the Conclave's intel severely underestimated the numbers of believers. He was rethinking his original plan to make the Sojourner the scapegoat for destroying the Conclave and considering how he could himself rule as the Sojourner. As he considered his options, he felt once more the conviction that the Man in the Sky wanted him to rule, that it had been the Sky's plan all along, that everything he had done had been foreordained by the deity. He found himself carried along with the idea of the original Sojourner that believing in the Man in the Sky was not religionism, that it was absolute fact. Religionism by definition meant believing in the unproven. As he wore the Sojourner's garb, he was coming to see that the Man in the Sky was real. He felt he could present the argument to his grandfather, that his grandfather would understand. When he ruled in place of the Conclave, he would do it in homage to his grandfather. As was often the case, thinking of his revered ancestor brought him nearly to tears.

The technician crouching on the floor, hearing the anguish in the speaker's voice, was convinced anew of the Sojourner's holy mission.

After finished the video, the Sojourner said a few approving words to the technician who was abasing himself in the approved manner. Regretfully Chandler put away the garments of the Sojourner and returned to his suite, exhausted.

The waiter from the pension had been watching and as the lights were extinguished in the penthouse, hurried to the service door of the lab, eager to retrieve the trolley and end the evening. He always waited for the lights to go out, if possible, because the guy from the Conclave, the councilor or whatever he was called, gave him the creeps. He had only interacted with him once or twice and the sneer and the fighting ball were both things he never wanted to see again.

The light from the elevator was bright enough that the waiter could gather up the dishes, noting with anticipation, the full open bottle of wine. He began to pull the trolley into the elevator, swearing at its weight, when he looked under the tablecloth and found one of the scientists passed out.

Promising himself to quit this job and return to civilization as soon as possible, he contemplated his options. This citizen had probably been drinking with the councilor and he wanted nothing to do with that personage. The scientists were notorious drunks and druggies, or so he'd been told. They certainly poured it down at the bar in the pension. Still they were good guys and decent tippers. He could wheel the trolley over to the office and someone would identify the citizen and then he would be stuck putting him to bed. That would take time and he had that open bottle of wine to think about.

The waiter, an experienced drinker himself, knew this drunk would likely not remember where he was when he passed out. Leaving him on the floor in the service kitchen was an option, but then he might still be there in the morning when the day staff delivered the morning meal. That would be a crappy thing to do to them. Upon brief reflection, the waiter wheeled the trolley into the lab area on the other side of the elevator and dumped the body onto the floor in one of the empty labs. Looking at the poor schlep spread out on the hard floor, he rolled up a few discarded lab coats and tucked them under his lolling head as a pillow. Between the hangover and sleeping on the lab floor, the waiter thought, he would feel really terrible in the morning.

34

At the moment the waiter saw the light go off in the penthouse, Piet and Arlo peered cautiously at the open parking lot from their vantage point on the second floor terrace of an abandoned restaurant. Arlo's map showed a central boulevard ending at a large plaza flanked by the facilities labeled Laboratory and Refinery. They had trudged in silence, following the central boulevard until they could see the plaza. Night had fallen and they were able to stay in shadow.

They climbed an outdoor staircase up to a terraced dining area that afforded a view of the entire plaza. Each of the two clusters of buildings was fronted by a large administration-type structure. Even without the map, identifying the building on their right as the refinery was easily done because of the banks of flood lights illuminating huge silver tanks behind the admin building. A few lights showed on the ground floor where workers were undoubtedly performing 24-hour maintenance.

The lab building was also mostly dark except for

security lights over the doorways. Dim work lights glowed in a few windows. The parking lot was in shadow but they could see numerous aircars at charging stations and a brightly lit hotel or restaurant a couple of blocks from their vantage point.

"This is definitely a Conclave operation," Piet nodded at the helicopter on the roof of the lab.

"Yeah, but what are they doing here?" Arlo asked. "I don't see any security. Want to go down to that restaurant and see what we can find out?"

Piet was amenable and they ambled the two blocks without meeting anyone. Like Colt, they noted the sign on the door. Inside they found a desk with a wall of keys and a bored receptionist watching a video. An old-fashioned elevator and staircase flanked the door to the dining room. They headed toward the dining room, when the receptionist woke up and said, "Hey, you guys need to sign in."

"We just got here," Piet said.

"Names." The receptionist looked at a list on his video screen.

Piet and Arlo gave him some names.

"You're not here." He flipped through a few more screens, then scowled. "Say, are you citizens with the plant? This pension is only for lab staff."

"Yeah, we're with the plant," Piet said.

"Well, you're in the wrong place. Those guys can't keep anything straight. And you can't go over there tonight because their dormitory is closed. You'll have to stay here. Mind sharing a room?"

They didn't and the receptionist seemed relieved. He handed them keys. "You better go get some chow," he nodded toward the restaurant, "the kitchen closes in a little while."

"What about the bar, Arlo asked.

He smirked, "oh, that stays open all night." He went back to his video.

While the food in the restaurant was free and good, the bar was cash only. The dining room had been almost completely empty and was self-service so there were no opportunities for gathering intel. The few late diners barely looked at them.

The bar was busier, and Piet thought they were getting a few inquiring looks. They moved up to the bar and complained loudly to the bartender about being sent to the wrong place.

"You're lucky," he replied, delivering drinks and a dish of nuts. "The quarters over there are just a barracks and you have to share them with the Conclave's militia, who are a surly group of citizens. If I was you I would try to get billeted over here. The food is better and, if you're thirsty, we're open as long as you want."

Piet looked around. "Are any of these citizens from the refinery? Someone who could give us the inside dope on the situation over there?"

"Actually, no. Not tonight. They had been working around the clock over there, gearing up for something, then a few days ago they shipped nearly everybody out, even most of the soldiers."

Arlo tried to sound disinterested. "So these citizens all work for the lab? What does it do anyway?"

"You got me," the bartender said. "The tall guy in the corner is one of the bosses. You could ask him."

Arlo began to turn his head, but Piet forestalled him. "Actually, we might do that another time. I'm really sleepy." He glanced at Arlo meaningfully.

"Drink up. We need to get some shut eye."

Arlo obliging downed his drink, and they strolled into the lobby. Once there, Piet made a sign for silence and gestured toward the stairs. They hurried to the landing; Piet stopped and watched the lobby.

Within a very short time, the tall guy the bartender had alluded to, emerged from the bar and approached the desk. They heard him asking the receptionist for their names and room number. He wanted details about their arrival and the citizen gave him what he knew, his tone respectful.

As the citizen disappeared through the front door, pulling a comm from his pocket, Piet hurried up the stairs looking for a back way out of the building. They quickly found service stairs at the rear of the building and hurried down to the back door and around the side of the building in time to see the tall guy crossing the parking lot, heading for the lab.

"He was giving us the stink eye back in the bar," Piet whispered as they watched their target pull something from his pocket and use it to open a door.

"I really want to go after him and find out who he is talking to."

"Looks like you need a key." Arlo said, unhelpfully.

"The parking lot's pretty dark. Let's use the aircars as cover and see if what we can find on the other side of the building." Piet crouched and ran, followed reluctantly by Arlo.

What they found on the other side of the building were a cluster of small outbuildings, a huge expanse of algae ponds, and several large, stainless steel tanks. They also found an ancient fire escape.

"Think it's safe?" Arlo asked.

"Only one way to find out. I'll boost you up."

While Arlo hung precariously from a rusty fire escape, Ana and Colt inadvertently got some quality sleep. Chandler lay in the darkness, making plans.

In a building that had once sold household goods, Jordi collapsed on a sofa. He was tired to death, but sleep was unsafe because surrounding him he could hear the whispers of the ghosts. Groggily he gathered a dusty pile of ancient pillows and coverlets and collapsed on the sofa, pulling them on top of his body and over his head. Only when he was completely covered did he fall into an exhausted sleep.

Arlo pulled himself onto the rusty platform of the ancient decrepit fire escape where a door, half paneled in glass, was set in the wall of building. He looked through the window but could see nothing except another wall. As he leaned against the door, it opened at his touch. Apparently Conclave security had dropped the ball on this entrance. Once inside, he found that the door opened into a stairwell. He hurried down the stairs where, as he expected, he found another door opening onto the back of the building a few steps away from where Piet stood, looking up.

When he heard the door open, Piet hurried over and together they entered the lab building. The back door opened into a corridor lined with offices and workrooms. They followed it toward the front of the building, hearing nothing. The corridor ended at a main reception area with a cross-corridor extending left and right away from the foyer. Hesitating for a moment, they both heard a noise coming from an office nearby and silently drifted toward the sound.

A sliver of light on the floor indicated which office the sound came from. The occupant, whom they assumed was the tall lab boss from the bar, was speaking into a comm.

He was describing them. "They don't look like artifact hunters. They said they were hired to work at the refinery." There was silence for a time then he said, "So they could be new guys for the plant?" He paused. "What do you mean, it doesn't matter? We've only filled two tanks." He listened some more then he said, sharply, "Tomorrow? When tomorrow?" There was a longer interval while the other party spoke at length. Then the boss said, "Does the citizen from the Conclave know what's going down?" Another pause. "Finally." And "No, no, we're ready." Piet and Arlo heard a chair squeak and the sliver of light vanished. They stepped back into the foyer, flattening against the wall but the citizen headed down the corridor away from them toward the refinery.

Arlo peeked around the corner watching as he followed the corridor almost to the end then turned left toward the back of the lab and vanished. Piet and Arlo hurried after him, stopping outside a reinforced steel door. Piet put his hand on the door, which felt warm. They could hear a faint humming sound as if heavy machinery was operating. The door was locked. A faint green light illuminated a key card slot. The corridor extended a few more feet toward an exterior door, unlocked, through which Piet and Arlo cautiously exited. They could now see that the lab and refinery buildings were connected by a sort of glass tunnel almost a story in height. Faint security lights set in its ceiling revealed several tubes running between the two structures.

Across the open space between the two buildings another door opened into the refinery. It too required a key card but someone had thoughtfully left one hanging from a nail.

As they were preparing to enter the building, they heard a strange whooshing sounding in the sky. Reflexively they looked up where they saw faint lights outlining a giant ovoid air ship heading over the city toward the coast.

Arlo, swearing, followed Piet through the door. Once there, they could go no farther. They were in a small anteroom. Opposite the door to the outside, a sign on another door informed them that access was restricted to authorized personnel only and that entry without a HAZMAT suit was forbidden. Lockers along one wall held white HAZMAT suits, rubber boots and gloves and plastic helmets with respirators. A clipboard with a signup sheet was meaningless except to indicate at least a dozen workers were employed.

"Do you need gear like this for refining petroleum from algae?" Arlo whispered to Piet, who snapped, "You're asking me?"

They carefully retreated into the space between the two buildings. Across the parking lot, the pension lights were almost completely dark as were lights in the lab and refinery buildings except for the dim security lights in the doorways. The parking lot was in shadow. Without the pall that hung over the city, the sky was luminous, stars shown brightly. Piet was tired of seeing the sky. He longed to return to the Subs.

They were both exhausted. The prudent course,

they agreed, was to get a few hours sleep in their room at the hotel.

35

When Colt awakened, he instantly thought of Ana and felt a surge of concern. Then he realized simultaneously that he had to empty his bladder immediately and that a small furry animal had died in his mouth whilst he slept.

The bladder problem was solved using one of the lab's sinks. He had a slight headache from the drug and felt less than sharp. And he was hungry.

He decided to return to the service kitchen and take his chances finding something to drink. He left the lab cautiously, but this floor was silent and appeared unused. He crossed the elevator to the door marked Private. Finding the little kitchen empty, he gratefully drank some water. The elegant dining room appeared to be empty also, the table set for one person. As he stepped into the room, automatically noting only one other door into the room, it opened and a citizen dressed as a waiter emerged.

"May I help you," he said, noting the lab coat, "are you Dr. Bede?"

"I'm Dr. Bede's husband."

The waiter looked him over. He seemed annoyed.

"Councilor Besdine didn't mention there were two guests," he grumped.

"That's Chandler. He always has a lot on his mind."

The waiter grimaced.

"Where is the Councilor, by the way?" Colt asked brightly.

"He was up early and went to a meeting. I was told to prepare breakfast for Dr. Bede when she awoke. I'll prepare another for you, if you'll give me a few minutes."

"No problem at all. I'll look forward to it." Colt went through the door to the penthouse turning to watch the waiter begin to lay out dishes for another place at the table.

The door into the penthouse opened onto another long corridor with doors on both sides. The second door on the left had a wedge stuck between the door and the carpet as a makeshift lock. Colt kicked it away, his heart quickening with anticipation.

Ana was still in bed, sitting up, brushing her hair. As he entered, she looked up, irritated, and said, "Can't you knock?" before registering that the citizen now entering her room was not Chandler but Colt.

She stopped brushing her hair and held her hands in front of her chest, shocked. "Am I dreaming?" she said.

Colt rushed across the room and put his arms around her. "It's me. I'm here," he muttered, idiotically.

They kissed. "You must be real," she said, "your breath smells like a sewer." She kissed him again.

They sat silently together for a few minutes, savoring the moment.

"We've got to do something," Ana finally said. "Chandler is culturing the plague."

"I know. I was listening to your conversation." He told her about the drugged bread pudding and she laughed.

"It knocked me out, too. I finally got some sleep."

"But we have to do something."

"What? Can the plague organism even be destroyed?"

"I don't know," Ana said, thoughtfully.

"You think about it while I take a shower and throw these clothes in the sanitizer."

Ana frowned, "He's pretending to be someone called the Sojourner. Do you know anything about that?"

"That's what Piet thought, but I didn't believe him."

"This is all just crazy. Why would he do that?"

"I don't know, but if it's Chandler, he has a plan. Let's talk about it later. We need to get dressed and get out of here."

When Colt returned from the sonic shower, clean and dressed in newly sanitized clothes, including his useful lab coat, he should have been thinking about plans to destroy the plague organism rather than how yummy Ana looked still sitting in bed, her hair hanging every which way.

Before he could become completely distracted, a soft knock sounded at the door. The waiter advised them that breakfast waited on their convenience in the dining room. He was returning to the pension, but, he added, if they needed anything, he could be reached via the intercom in the service kitchen. And no, he responded to Colt's question, he had no idea how long Councilor Besdine would be in his meeting. He seemed to imply there was no accounting for what Councilor Besdine might do.

While Ana had her own sonic shower and dressed, Colt contacted Piet and was advised that Piet and Arlo were right across the parking lot. They had gone downstairs for breakfast in the pension and no one had seemed to notice them. They reported an air of expectation in the breakfast crowd, a lot of whispering and animated conversations. Something was apparently up. They would do nothing until they heard from Colt.

In the dining room, the waiter had set out a selection of covered dishes. While Ana picked over the offerings, Colt grabbed some food and made a sandwich. He was anxious to examine the penthouse and worried that Chandler might return at any moment. Ana had reported entering the suite via a different elevator than the one in the kitchen and he wanted to locate it and any other entrances.

He went down the corridor away from the dining room. He passed several doors that opened onto what appeared to be guest rooms. One door, however, was different from the rest. It was inlaid with myriad small pieces of wood and metal arranged in an intricate, polychrome design. Behind the door, Colt found several beautiful rooms decorated in an unusual style featuring sumptuous wall hangings, soft couches, and numerous gilded mirrors. Since mirrors were proscribed under the New Dispensation, seeing himself repeatedly replicated was unsettling. He was not accustomed to thinking about how he appeared to other citizens although he knew they found him attractive. He stopped before one large mirror and took a good look. He didn't care for the unfamiliar feeling of seeing another self looking back.

Finally he came to a small room with yet another large mirror and several wardrobes holding long white hooded robes. He had found the dressing room of the Sojourner.

Colt peeked into the next room that was set up for recording videos. A second door was inset with a security screen that showed another elevator.

Leaving the Sojourner's suite, Colt found yet another elevator at the end of a small corridor. He took the elevator to the ground floor, where, as he had assumed, it opened into the lobby of the building. He contacted Piet, who was waiting nearby for his call, and within a short time Piet and Arlo entered the lobby. A receptionist emerged from a small office and took his place behind a tall counter, enquiring politely but indifferently whether he could be of assistance. Colt replied in the negative, and the receptionist returned to the little office.

When Piet and Arlo arrived, Colt waved them over to the elevator, and they swiftly rose to the penthouse level. He briefly explained the need for caution since Chandler might return at any moment, noting that there seemed little concern for security. Piet was gratified when Colt immediately asked about Beau's condition.

They met with Ana in the dining room. She and Arlo embraced. Then Arlo said, "Let's get Ana out of here to safety. We can head back through the dead city and wait for Old Matley to pick her up."

But Ana said adamantly, "I'm not leaving until we do something about the plague organism Chandler is culturing in the algae beds."

This news shocked them.

"Why would he do that?" Piet was aghast.

"I think he's planning to use it against the Conclave," Ana said.

"Retribution," Arlo nodded. "Many people believe the Conclave initiated the original plague. Maybe Chandler believes this would be repayment in kind."

"Whatever it is, we can't let it happen," Piet said. "I'm no fan of the Conclave, but they are better than the chaos that would follow on their destruction."

"I expect Chandler thinks he will take over for the Conclave," Colt said. "He'll blame the destruction of the Conclave on the Sojourner and his followers and he will take the place of the Conclave."

Arlo whistled. "Clever and it might work."

"We can't let it work," Ana said. "You cannot control the plague. The plague organisms don't live very long but the disease spreads quickly from person to person, and there is no cure."

"Have you figured out a way to destroy the plague organisms before they can be dispersed?" Colt asked Ana.

"Depriving them of oxygen and exposing them to extremely high temperatures are the only methods I can think of to destroy them. Developing a vaccine that would immunize citizens might not be possible and, if it were, would take time and research."

"I don't think we have much time at all," Piet said. "Something is going on today or tomorrow. The citizens at the pension were excited this morning." He told them about the conversation he and Arlo had overheard the previous evening.

"We need help and we need intel," Colt said.

"I can get us help," Piet said, "but how are we going to get intel? We can't just waltz in and start asking questions. We don't know enough."

"Ana could," Arlo said. "She speaks their language."

Colt gave him a dirty look. "I don't want Ana to expose herself any more than is necessary. Before we do anything, I have an idea."

He explained his plan and Piet said, "You do it. You've got the magic lab coat."

Colt once again took the elevator to the lobby and when the receptionist again emerged from his cubbyhole, Colt said, "Can you ask Healer Bruxton to join us in the Councilor's suite?"

"I'll buzz him." The citizen returned to his office, and Colt hurried to the elevator, anxious to avoid alerting the healer. He needn't have worried. At least fifteen minutes passed before they heard the elevator doors open and Bruxton hurried down the hallway, looking important, carrying his black satchel with the silver healer sigil. He stopped short when he saw the party who had gathered in the dining room. When he stepped through the doorway, Arlo stepped behind him and closed the door loudly.

Colt began in a congenial tone.

"Healer Bruxton, you are an old acquaintance of myself and my wife." He nodded toward Ana, who made a short unsmiling bow.

"These other two citizens are Piet Lem, chief of Grupo Uno in the city, and Arlo Gauss, also of the city." Piet and Arlo raised their fists for bumping. The healer put his satchel on a chair and responded with impressive gusto.

Colt spoke softly. "We are here to collect my wife and ensure that she returns to the city safely. We summoned you because we are interested in your motivations for kidnapping her and murdering our good friend Citizen Petrie."

Lulled by Colt's tone, the healer took a moment to assimilate the accusation. He drew back protectively and began fiddling with the omnipresent amber beads.

"I had to," he said.

"Also," Piet said, "we are interested in your participation in culturing the plague organism."

Bruxton looked worried. "I have nothing to do with that. The Conclave directed production of a batch for research purposes."

"Ridiculous!" Ana snapped. "There's more than enough to infect a city."

"Talk to Councilor Besdine. He's director of lab and refinery activities." He added, in a pompous tone, "I'm here in another capacity entirely."

"To wait on the Sojourner," Arlo said.

"To serve the Sojourner," Bruxton corrected, adding, "I have that honor."

"You do know that Councilor Besdine and the Sojourner are one and the same," Colt said.

"That is not possible." Bruxton said, offended.

"Have you ever seen the Sojourner unmasked?" Colt asked.

"No. It's forbidden. To look on the face of the Sojourner is to die instantly because he is not an ordinary citizen. He is a direct extension of the Man in the Sky. I've seen it happen."

"In person?" Arlo said.

"No, in videos. Also, I've seen the Sojourner and Councilor Besdine talking together. The Sojourner is staying here at the Councilor's invitation."

"You're telling me that Chandler Besdine is a religionist, a follower of the Man in the Sky?" Piet laughed.

"No, not exactly. The Councilor is just more open-minded than the Conclave. He doesn't believe in persecuting religionists."

"So what is the Sojourner doing here in the dead city? What are his plans?" Piet asked.

Bruxton chose that moment to sit on one of the chairs and crossed his arms comfortably.

"The Sojourner is here for an extended period of meditation. He receives his instructions from the Sky. When he was forced to leave the city, he was told to come here and await orders. That's all I know."

"You're not here alone. He must have followers." Arlo coaxed.

"A very small group is here working in the refinery. Most of the equipment is automated so few workers are needed. I'm only here because the Sojourner sent out word that he wanted to see Dr. Bede." Here Bruxton nodded to Ana. "He said he had important information for her that he needed to deliver in person. Of course, it is an honor to meet with the Sojourner."

"And the Sojourner told you to kill Teegan?" Ana snapped.

"No. The Sojourner said he wanted to see Dr. Bede alone. Teegan was just unfortunately in the way. I thought about bringing her to the dead city but I knew she would make trouble." His ingratiating smile was replaced by one of extreme anger.

"You found out she wasn't a serious religionist, did you? She was just trying it on for size." Arlo said. "And you, she was just trying you on for size, too. She probably wanted to know what it was like to sleep with someone fat."

The pudgy healer snarled and took a step toward Arlo.

"Enough," Colt snapped.

The pudgy healer fought to control his emotions as Piet said, "The Conclave does not condone murder," adding parenthetically, "with the possible exception of religionists. That's why they invented the stasis chamber."

Bruxton got control of himself, assuming a smirk that dismissed the Conclave. "The Sojourner and his followers don't answer to the Conclave. Citizens may die now, but, when the Conclave is no more, the Man in the Sky will replace it and reign in perfect peace."

"And that will happen soon?" Piet asked.

"In the Sky's time. But yes, we expect it to be soon."

"So," Colt said, "the Man will come down from the Sky and decimate the Conclave?" He knew this was not the plan from conversations with Oren but he wanted to find out what this follower of the Sojourner would say.

The follower said, "Oh, no. He cannot come to rule in peace until his followers have subdued the Conclave. We must pave the way."

"And you plan to do this with conventional arms?" Piet queried.

"Of course. How else?" Bruxton looked puzzled.

"The personages in the Conclave and consistory will have to die?" Piet continued.

"Unless they surrender to the Sojourner. That's the way it works in war."

"The Conclave have lots of troops protecting themselves and the Citadel. They won't be easy to conquer."

"Yes, citizen Lem," the healer said smugly, "but we have the power of the Sky on our side."

"I see. You must have some soldiers to attack the Citadel, even with the power of the Sky." Piet gave himself silent props for managing to say this with a straight face.

"I'm sure we do. I believe some of our militias have been active in other parts of the planet."

"Not very successfully if the protestors in the city are an example," Colt said.

"That was a setback, but the Sojourner escaped. He said we were betrayed."

"Is it possible the Sojourner has troops bivouacked on one of the nearby floating islands?" Piet asked. Colt shot him a glance, intrigued by the idea.

"Possibly," Bruxton looked bored. "I'm not a soldier."

Colt changed topic. "The Sojourner doesn't have much security here in the dead city." Colt observed. "Neither does the refinery."

The healer said dismissively, "Why would they need security. There's nothing here to steal except tanks of fuel. The only approach is by sea and an old highway that connects to the city. Other than that, there's nothing around here but algae ponds. A few unsanctioned citizens hide in the little forest between here and the town of Deep Cove but the refinery workers are armed."

"How do they bring in supplies?" Arlo asked.

"They use conventional trucks to bring in supplies via the road and aircars can also come up the coast. There's just enough beach from Deep Cove for aircars to operate."

"What about the airships?" Colt asked.

"Now those are myths." The little healer said decisively. "I know some of the less educated citizens claim to have seen them at night, but we know they don't exist. They must have seen helicopters."

"I noticed a helicopter on the roof," Piet said.

Bruxton sniffed. "That's Councilor Besdine's personal vehicle, for consulting with the Conclave. He flies it himself."

"Councilor Chandler is a talented citizen," Arlo commented, enjoying the healer's scowl.

36

Meanwhile, Councilor Besdine was coming to the end of his patience. The meeting with the lab staff was not going according to his plan; his plans, so near fruition, were being stymied at every turn. Now the plague organism was ready to be harvested ahead of schedule, and the moon-busters were only half built. At least now that he finally had Ana, he could proceed with arming the powerful weapons. He had no doubt she would aid him, or he would turn her into a baked potato.

Events would move forward at an accelerated pace after he dealt with this cadre of rebellious scientists. He wished he could just execute them now, but he needed them to harvest the plague organisms. Once that was done, they were expendable. He entertained himself with plans to drop them off on one of the uninhabited floating islands and forget about them.

But now six young scientists, the senior members of the group who had been charged with culturing the plague organisms, all solemnly dressed in white lab coats, sat around a conference table. They had been chosen for their youth and lack of connections in the Conclave. Although their training had been at one of the lesser research institutes far from the Citadel, they were all competent to follow the directions for culturing the plague Chandler had recovered from among his grandfather's papers.

Chandler's ancestor had been a prominent member of the board of directors and a generous financial supporter of the non-governmental organization, the NGO, that transformed itself into the Conclave. The plague had been originated in a private lab funded and operated by the NGO. As a function of their dedication to helping populations who were victims of famine and disease, often, but not always, as a result of natural catastrophes, their scientists had been working to produce a programmable pest killer that would stop the cycle of introducing a new species to control pests, which, once the pests were eradicated, became themselves an invasive species which required introduction of controlling organisms, and so on in infinite progression. The scientists were finally successful. Several invasive species of pests were successfully eradicated from croplands and bodies of water with the organism they created in their lab. By design the organisms interfered with the reproductive cycle of pests, and they could not reproduce themselves. After a short interval of potency, they died. The perfect solution.

While fine-tuning the organisms, the scientists realized, after a series of unfortunate mishaps, that the organisms would also eradicate citizens.

As more and more often the conditions they tried

to ameliorate arose from overpopulation, the board of directors of the NGO saw the organisms as offering an opportunity to reduce some of the overpopulation. With overpopulation under control, an enlightened group of citizens could initiate reforms for the wellbeing of the planet and its remaining population. Many directors of the organization had read and been intrigued by the theories of a scientific philosopher named Johannes Zapf-Gauss who advocated a strong, planet-wide central government and postulated several needed societal modifications such as eradication of religionism and demystification of sexuality. Citizens' loyalties would lie with the central governing body, a group epitomized by wisdom and philanthropy.

Chandler's ancestor had become unhinged when he realized his fellow board members were using the organisms to commit mass murder, genocide. They had renamed themselves the Conclave of Elders and were planning to rule under a New Dispensation modeled after the writings of Zapf-Gauss.

As director of the laboratory that developed the organism, Chandler's ancestor felt profoundly guilty and vowed to destroy the instructions for its culture. Although ostensibly maintaining his position in the Conclave, he secretly vowed to destroy the Conclave. As an elder, he joined with the faction within the Conclave who became convinced that deep science, or ephemerist thought, such as that of Zapf-Gauss, should be banned.

Chandler smiled inwardly. Of course, the perfect solution had not been so perfect. Many of the women who survived the plague were unable to bring an infant to term. Just as the organism could not replicate itself, the same effect was introduced into its hosts. The population of the planet was steadily dropping below replacement levels.

Coming out of his reverie, Chandler listened to the chief scientist, a young female citizen with red hair and a gauche, belligerent affect, finish up a long report on the successful cultivation process and the optimum remaining time until harvest.

That process was nearly at an end. A large quantity was almost ready to be pumped from the algae beds. But the scientists were having qualms about the volume of plague organisms.

Chandler indulged her even though he knew what was in the report. Unfortunately she had begun to question the orders from the Conclave with respect to the size of the sample the Conclave's scientists needed for their research.

"Preliminary tests indicate the sample needed for research purposes is several magnitudes less than the requested quantity," she said, scowling. "It is difficult for us to envision a research project that would utilize the amounts requisitioned." She continued at length outlining possible research scenarios, none of which required vast quantities of plague organisms.

She waved her notes at him in an irritating manner.

Chandler had years to practice remaining calm and impassive in the face of the smarmy bombast of the elders. This citizen was no match for a self-important functionary from the highest level of the Conclave.

The other members of the staff were either watching the chief scientist or looking elsewhere. None seemed inclined to make eye contact with the representative of the Conclave. Still they were raising questions about the Conclave's orders and that meant they were seriously concerned.

"I am not a scientist, citizens. I have no conception of the goals of the Conclave's other scientists. Like you, I am here to follow their orders." Chandler had reiterated some variation on this speech at various times during the meeting.

"I don't share your concerns, citizen scientists. The organisms are short-lived. If they are not used quickly by the Conclave's scientists at the Citadel, they will die. Perhaps the Conclave's scientists have found a way to preserve the organisms, flash freeze them, for instance. Otherwise all that happens is energy and resources are wasted, unfortunate, but not a tragedy."

"Transporting such a large volume is dangerous," she protested.

Chandler decided to ignore her. He rose, "Besides, I am here to do the Conclave's bidding, as are you. They wanted this quantity of organisms and that is what they will get." His pale blue velvet eyes were suddenly flat and implacable.

The young citizens stirred nervously. Their young leader looked to them anxiously for support; all but one avoided her gaze. He looked at her grimly and gave his head a microscopic, warning shake.

Unhappily, she gathered up her papers and hurried from the room.

The other young scientists trailed after her.

Chandler waited until they had disappeared from view then left himself, glad to be done with them but still worried about their commitment. He had planned to return to his quarters and instead decided to go down to the pump room to ensure that the foreman understood his orders.

Harvesting the plague organisms was a hazardous undertaking. The foreman and workers in the pump room were selected from the Sojourner's more fanatical followers and presumably would obey instructions from the Sojourner without requiring tedious explanations. Chandler was indifferent to their safety, but they had been supplied with coveralls and respirators that might protect them from the organisms.

Chandler wanted to make sure they were on board with his agenda. As soon as the scientists advised him that the organisms had reached potency, they would immediately be pumped into one of the stainless steel tanks to be transported by a powerful transport helicopter. The Sojourner's followers had been told that the organisms were to be used for research.

In fact the organisms would be seeded in the Conclave's water supply and deposited on the gardens surrounding the Citadel where food was grown for the Conclave's tables. Chandler had a remote control that would release the organisms from the transport ship so he would have the satisfaction of delivering death to the Conclave himself.

37

Jordi was wandering disconsolately through the streets of the dead city looking for something to eat. His aircar, or rather the aircar he had taken from Rick back in Deep Cove, had disappeared. He assumed Rick had managed to recall it. He was thirsty, too. He had gagged down some of the thick slimy rainwater from some old fountains, but it was not enough. His hair and clothes were filthy. Inwardly, he was awash in despair and self-loathing. Finally it had come to him that he must kill himself. Despite the commands of the Conclave, he must suicide.

But how? He prowled the streets, becoming more aware of hunger and thirst. His head buzzed with disjointed commands, to take his pistol and put a bullet into his brain, to return to the seashore and throw himself into the water to drown or be eaten by sea monsters, to hang himself from one of the wrought iron balconies that rimmed the squares. He was not so much walking as staggering forward on his tiptoes when he emerged into a large square. Across from him, on the other side of the open space, two large buildings were connected by a huge glass tube. Away to his left, he could see a smattering of aircars. Occasionally citizens would cross the square and enter one of the buildings. No one paid attention to him. He staggered into the square, looking for a café. There should be a café, he thought, where he could get water, food. At that moment a citizen in a uniform of some sort began to walk toward him, causing the buzzing in his head to increase, building fear. He tried to turn, to run away, but he caught his foot on a cobblestone and fell to his knees. He began scrabbling in his pocket for his pistol.

The citizen reached him before he could secure his weapon.

"Buddy," the citizen said. "Are you okay? Let me help you up."

He held out a hand to Jordi, who started at it.

"C'mon," the citizen reached down and grabbed Jordi's arm, pulling him to his feet.

"Water," Jordi whispered.

"Lets go over to the pension and get you something to drink."

"And eat," Jordi said. "Food."

The citizen smiled. "And something to eat," he said.

He half carried Jordi across the square to the pension, helping him into the foyer. The citizen was not tall but felt sturdy and reassuring.

"What's this?" the desk clerk asked.

"Some artifact hunter, I guess." Jordi's rescuer said. "They don't come prepared."

He led Jordi toward the back of the hotel, to the dining room, where he helped Jordi to a chair then quickly returned with a glass of water.

Jordi drank it off, holding out the glass for more, but the citizen shook his head, "don't overtax your stomach all of a sudden," he said. "I'll get you some soup." He returned shortly with a bowl of soup, Jordi had no idea what kind it was, but it tasted delicious.

Sated for the moment, he thanked the friendly citizen. He could see that the uniform the citizen wore was not military but one worn by laborers or factory workers.

"Relax for a minute and if you can handle it I'll bring you some more food."

Jordi let himself relax.

"I needed water," he said. "All I could find was rainwater in the fountains." He felt his head nod. "It tasted awful."

The stranger laid the back of his hand against Jordi's forehead. His skin felt too warm.

"Let's get you upstairs. You need to lie down."

Jordi obediently stood up, swaying, and let the citizen help him up the stairs and into a bedroom where he slumped onto the bed.

"I'm going to summon a healer," the citizen said. "You've got a fever, probably from drinking bad water."

"Healer," Jordi said, stirring. "Got to kill the healer."

The citizen gave Jordi an assessing look. He had noted the pistol but assumed it was for protection. Most of the artifact hunters, the smart ones, carried weapons.

Back in Chandler's quarters, Colt was thinking about what to do with the healer. Chandler might return at any moment and they needed to get Ana to safety. At the moment, he did not want Chandler to know about their presence and he was sure the healer would go directly to Chandler if they let him loose.

At that moment, the healer's comm buzzed and, before Colt could grab it, the healer put it to his ear. He listened briefly then switched it off.

"I have to go. Some artifact hunter got fever from drinking bad water and they've put him to bed in the pension."

Ana looked at Colt mouthing 'Jordi?'

Shrugging, Colt nodded to Piet and Arlo. "We'll go with you," he said, "We're done here for the time being."

The healer recovered his satchel and hurried out, the others following. Colt let them get ahead and whispered to Ana, "You saw Jordi?"

"I didn't get a chance to tell you. He came to the healer's cottage in Rick's aircar. I think it was programmed to come here, but . . ." She was going to say more, but Colt forestalled her.

"I know all about that. Did the healer see Jordi?"

"No, Jordi was hiding in the shed when the healer came to get me. I think he's gone crazy. He's determined to kill the healer in revenge for Teegan."

"Jordi killed Oren and Linnet. He has developed an obsession about religionists."

"Poor Linnet wasn't a religionist," Ana protested.

"He thought she was. He isn't rational. We need to keep him from killing the healer."

"Why?" Ana said. "Bruxton killed Teegan."

"Because revenge never ends it. We need to get Jordi back to the city where Yonatan can help him."

By this time they had reached the pension.

Bruxton sketched a salute to the receptionist, apparently he was known here, and headed upstairs followed by Colt and Ana. Arlo and Piet went into the bar, which was empty except for the bored-looking bartender.

"Kinda quiet," Piet said, seating himself at the bar. Arlo seated himself where he could watch the door.

"Something's going on. The guys who work in the pump house are on duty." The bartender set out two glasses and, at Piet's suggestion, poured one for himself.

A group of youngsters in lab coats came in and seated themselves at a large table in the corner.

One of them detached himself and approached the bar, placing an order for wine. He turned to Piet, "Who are you?" he said.

"I might ask you the same thing," Piet replied.

The kid made a face. "Sorry," he said. "I'm on edge. You're new here."

"My friend and I," he nodded to Arlo, "are supposed to be working in the Refinery but our orders haven't come through."

"I thought they had discontinued the refinery operations," the kid said indifferently. He took a carafe of wine from the bartender and Piet picked up the tray of glasses, following the kid to the round table and taking a seat. No one seemed to notice.

"My friend and I are concerned," Piet frowned, "if the refinery is closed, why were we sent here? Will we be out of a job?"

"Don't know. Just a typical screw up, I guess. You can hang around for a day or two and ride out of here with us."

"Maybe once we're gone, the refinery operations

will resume," another kid offered.

"You're not with the refinery, then," Piet sipped his drink.

"No. We're here doing research for the Conclave. Our work here will be complete tomorrow." They drank in silence. Piet noticed that they were all extremely young.

Finally, a female citizen with unusual red hair, tapped her finger emphatically on the notebook in front of her and said, "I'm still worried about the guys operating the pumps."

"You don't think they know what they're doing," someone said reasonably.

"You've talked to them. They're not trained. The only one who knows anything is the foreman."

The rest of the young lab workers seemed indifferent.

"How many technicians work in the pump facility?" Piet asked idly.

One of the youngsters answered automatically, "Two and the foreman."

"Who are you?" the red haired one snapped, noticing him for the first time.

Piet gave her the story about the missing orders.

"Typical," she muttered. "But once the research project is complete and the fuel stored in the two tanks is transported, they may resume the refining process. It will take some time for the algae beds to be ready though."

"I guess I'm confused. We thought the refinery was fully operational," Piet said. Furthermore, he had no idea how the refining process worked or about growing algae, for that matter.

"We've been using the algae beds for . . . ," one of

the kids began helpfully.

"Research. We've been doing some research for the Conclave of Elders." The citizen with the red hair interrupted. She looked around and stressed the end of her statement.

"Right," the kid muttered and the others nodded agreement.

Colt and Ana followed Bruxton into a room at the top of the stairs. Jordi, looking very ill, lay on the bed, thrashing restlessly as a stout man in a workman's uniform tried to put wet rags on his forehead. He looked up anxiously when they entered. Jordi's pistol and comm were in plain sight on the bedside table.

"Healer Bruxton, thank you for coming. I found this citizen in the square. He said he drank from the fountains." They fist bumped. The stout man looked surprised at the presence of Colt and Ana but he fist bumped Colt and nodded to Ana.

"This citizen is our friend," Colt explained. We planned to meet here but we lost communications."

The stout citizen nodded, "The comms don't always work."

"We have business with Councilor Besdine," Ana smiled.

Bruxton meanwhile had been caring for Jordi, administering medication for the fever. Finally, he pulled a sheet of patches from his satchel and placed one on Jordi's neck.

"That will knock him out for a few hours. He should be good as new when it wears off." Before he could return them to his satchel, Colt took the sheet from his hand.

"How strong are these things?" he said, pretending

to read the instructions. "Shouldn't you use two?"

The healer tried to grab the sheet. "Who's the healer here," he snapped. "They are very strong. They'll keep him under for several hours while he heals."

Before the healer could protest, Colt had peeled one of the patches and stuck it on his neck. The healer tried to raise his hands to peel it off but Colt held his wrists until he started to sway, then pushed him in chair. Very shortly he was asleep.

The good Samaritan looked at Colt and Ana fearfully.

Colt pulled a second patch from the sheet and stuck it on the healer's neck.

"That's too many. He might not wake up." The citizen made a gesture as if to remove the second patch.

Colt looked at him and he dropped his hands then raised them palms out in a defensive gesture.

"Leave him. He'll be okay." Colt said. "Now, tell me what you do here in the dead city."

He worked in the refinery. He explained that the refinery had been shut down after two of the three stainless steel tanks had been filled. Typically, once filled, a tank would be airlifted by one of the Conclave's heavy-duty helicopters and transported to the Citadel. This refinery had been set up to provide fuel exclusively for the use of the Conclave at the Citadel, he said proudly.

Sometime previously the procedure had changed. Two of the tanks were full and word had come from the Conclave via Councilor Besdine that operations would be paused. All the other refinery workers had been let go except himself who had remained to keep the facility secure. He monitored the pressure in the tanks and generally kept the place clean. He also monitored the pumping system to ensure that the tubes didn't become clogged. When the algae was ripe for processing into fuel, the top layer would be suctioned into the refinery, processed, then transferred to the tanks through a system of pipes. Some lizards had miraculously found a way to live off the algae around the edges of the beds and occasionally one would fall in and clog a tube. In answer to Ana's question, he said the pumps would be reversed to blow out the clog.

He had been told that the scientists were using the algae beds as part of a research project for the Conclave but he didn't know the details. It was almost over, was all he knew.

"Can you operate the pumps by yourself?" Ana asked.

Well, yes, he could. But he was not assigned that task. Workers had been brought in with the scientists to operate the pumping station. He sounded a little pissed off. No, he responded to Colt's question, he didn't know why they brought in their own people when he was completely competent to do it himself.

Colt had gone to the window to look across the parking lot at the two facilities. He was concerned about Chandler's whereabouts.

Ana was saying to the citizen, "I think they did you a favor. You're sure you don't know anything about the research project?"

The citizen shook his head, increasingly distressed. Then she turned to Colt, "I think we're going to need this citizen's assistance."

Colt looked interested. "You got an idea?" he said.

She nodded.

"I'm going downstairs to check in with Piet and Arlo," Colt said. "Wait a few minutes and join me."

"Are you armed?" he asked the citizen, who shook his head. He nodded toward Jordi's pistol and told Ana to bring it with her. He grinned. "You may need it," he said.

The citizen stared at Ana as she took the pistol. "What's going on?" he said to her. He was almost in tears.

38

In the foyer, the receptionist had abandoned his post and retreated to his little office, apparently napping.

Arlo looked up when Colt entered the bar and jerked his head to the corner of the room where Piet was seated with a group of kids in white lab coats.

Colt sauntered over to the group, leaning languidly against the wall.

"Citizen scientists," he nodded genially, positioning himself so he could see the door.

"We were just discussing the research project instituted by Councilor Besdine on behalf of the Conclave," Piet said.

"I didn't know Councilor Besdine was a scientist," Colt said.

The red-haired citizen snorted but said nothing. A couple of the boys just grinned.

"They think the Councilor may have misinterpreted the Conclave's requirements," Piet continued.

The scientists looked at each other, suddenly,

belatedly, wondering where this was going, who were these strangers.

"They are concerned about the volume of plague organisms they have been culturing in the algae beds." Piet sounded matter of fact.

The scientists all looked startled and then, taking a good look at Piet and Colt, afraid.

"As they well should be," said Ana, coming into the room and standing next to Colt, Jordi's rescuer trailing behind.

The red-haired scientist started to say one thing, then stood up, "You're Ana Bede," she said, "from the Institute of Temporal Epistemology. You worked with Prof. Elvistine—on the portal. I saw you speak at a symposium." The young scientists all looked impressed.

"Tell me," Ana looked around the table, "just how close are the organisms to being at full potency?"

The young citizen hesitated, then said, "Actually, we could harvest them immediately."

"Councilor Besdine plans to siphon the organisms into the remaining tank and transport it to the Conclave." Ana continued. "How many people would it kill if it were dumped on the Citadel and the countryside around it?"

Aghast, one of the youngsters said, "All of it? Tens of thousands of citizens, maybe more." They all looked shocked.

Ana continued, "What would happen if you pumped the fuel from the two tanks onto the algae beds?"

"And set them on fire," Arlo said, with gusto.

"You wouldn't need to set them on fire," one young scientist said contemptuously. "The fuel would deprive them of oxygen and they would die quickly. But why would you do that?"

"To keep Councilor Besdine from dropping them on the Conclave," Ana said.

"Why would he do that? He's a member of the Conclave," one of the kids protested.

"Besides," another added, clearly appalled, "he couldn't be sure of infecting just the Conclave. Other citizens would be infected also."

"We don't know the councilor's motivations, but we know he is planning to destroy the Conclave by unleashing the plague. He may see it as just retribution for some imagined wrongs to him and his family. Plus we know he is posing as a religionist called the Sojourner. We think he is planning to destroy the Conclave and take the planet for himself."

"Councilor Besdine can't be a religionist," one of the kids gasped, "He's a member of the Conclave of Elders. They aren't allowed to be religionists."

Standing at the back of the room, Jordi's good Samaritan stirred at these words.

"She didn't say he was a religionist," Arlo snapped. "She said he was posing as one."

"This is crazy." One of the kids pulled out a comm. Before he could activate it, Piet said, "put that away." When the kid hesitated, Piet reached across the table and snatched it from his hand.

They all looked shocked. This movement was their first indication that the strangers would actually take action against them, possibly put them in danger.

Piet handed the comm to Colt, who studied the display. "So you're the Councilor's spy in this little group. I wondered." He removed the power crystal and returned the comm. The others in the group glared at the spy, who said, "I never told him nothing. It was just some extra cash."

"He knows the organisms are ready?" Colt asked.

"He knows because we told him in a meeting this morning," the red-haired citizen said.

"We need to stop the harvesting of the organisms," Ana said. "And they need to be destroyed."

"You can't do that," one of the kids protested. "All that work. . . ."

"The Councilor will stop you," the spy said. "He has troops."

He would have said more, but they all glared at him. One of them called him a name.

"So do we," Piet said easily, pulling out his comm.

Then everyone looked at him.

Chandler returned to his penthouse suite and found that Ana was gone. He had taken a chance that she would awaken and find a way out of the building but without help she couldn't get far. He had counted on forcing her to assist in building several more moon-blasters but he couldn't worry about Ana Bede at the moment.

He called the pumping station where the scientists should be initiating the harvest but there was no answer. He had ordered the organisms harvested within the next few hours. Once the tank was filled, he would airlift it with his helicopter, the tank had been modified with a remote controlled rotating nozzle that would drop down and spray fine droplets of the plague organisms over a wide area. He would begin with the Citadel and his revenge would be realized. He could now feel the Man in the Sky speaking to him, empowering him to destroy the Conclave and assume control of the planet. As Sojourner, he could use the religionists, order them to fight under the direction of his personal troops, who were strategically located where they could attack the planet's large population centers. He had control of several of the airships, which Conclave scientists had recently perfected, and several moon blasters. He had always known he was special, his ancestor had assured him that he was chosen to destroy the Conclave. His ancestor had envisioned the planet descending into a kind of anarchy. With the Conclave gone, the centers of learning, the laboratories, would fade away, work on reversing the fertility problems would end. In a few generations, the planet would revert to a pristine world flourishing with plants and animals. A paradise.

But Chandler now saw that his grandfather's vision was too narrow. It lacked grandeur. He would surpass it and himself make the planet a paradise. He and the Man in the Sky.

With the Conclave and Consistory destroyed, with the personal army he had gathered augmented with his hordes of mindlessly obedient religionists, he would prevail.

Exhilarated, he gazed through the window of his penthouse, looking across the parking lot to the fields in the distance. On the other side of the fields lay the city. It was to be one of his first prizes of war. He would immediately destroy the Institute of Temporal Epistemology—he laughed to himself at Ana's ridiculous story about the portal—did she think him that credulous? Then he would flood the Subs, the city's vast anarchic underbelly, with poison gas and purify it once and for all.

Suddenly he heard a thunderous noise from the sky. Alarmed, he watched a huge troop-transport helicopter bearing the sigil of the Conclave land and armed mercenaries pour out, lining up at attention outside the hotel. Before his eyes, the first helicopter immediately departed and within minutes another, also loaded with troops, landed. As the second group joined the first, a figure glided from the hotel to be met by one of the soldiers. As they fist bumped, Chandler was consumed with fury. Even at this distance he recognized Piet Lem's effortless walk.

He knew instantly they had somehow penetrated his plan to release the plague. Infuriated, he gathered a few things together and headed for the heliport on top of the building. So be it. He would have to conquer the Conclave the old fashioned way. . . through war.

39

As Piet stood consulting with the commander of the mercenaries, they heard Chandler's helicopter start and begin to rise into the sky. They stood by helplessly as it flew toward the sea.

Piet had been in contact with the commander of the mercenaries since he had arrived in Deep Cove. They were still under orders to extirpate the Sojourner, who Piet had advised them was in the dead city. Once they learned about the project to culture the plague organism, word rapidly spread up the chain of command to the Conclave.

Colt, Piet, and Arlo left Ana with the young scientists who, once they got over complaining about all the work they had done, were happy to share with her the details of the culturing project.

Ana found that the extremely complicated directions for culturing the organism had been released to them at each stage of the process by a citizen identified as one of the Conclave's functionaries. Once each stage was successfully under way, the directions were returned to the functionary. The scientists all assured her that no one had copied the directions, that none of them had the complete set. They knew the danger, they assured her. She doubted they even now really understood the horrible possibilities of the thing.

They continued to insist that they were working for the Conclave, that Councilor Besdine would be vindicated. Only the entrance of the Conclave's representative, a very grand personage indeed, and a very angry one, caused real consternation among them.

The personage, himself, supervised the release of the fuel onto the algae beds and set the young scientists to work testing to ensure that the organisms were destroyed.

Later, when the excitement had died down, Ana took the red haired scientist and withdrew into a far section of the bar. The young citizen looked warily at the famous personage; in her world Ana Bede was an icon.

"What's you name," Ana asked gently.

"Dorcas. Dorcas Wovoka."

They chatted for a few minutes on topics of mutual interest, where Dorcas had studied and taken advanced degrees, which crèche she had been reared in. Ana found that Dorcas had been selected for training at one of the Conclave's elite academies. She outlined for Ana the course of study and proudly detailed some of her awards. She also noted that that the type of work required to culture the plague organism was not her primary focus. She had been a last minute replacement for another scientist. Her primary focus was fusion energy.

Ana then asked some technical questions about the process for culturing the plague virus, nodding as the young scientist responded.

Ana said, "You seem to have a good handle on the procedures."

"I guess." Dorcas fiddled with a saltshaker.

"It's pretty complicated." Ana observed.

"Very." The young citizen looked directly at Ana, adding, "very very complicated."

Ana paused.

"I think you could replicate the process yourself, though. I think you have an exceptional memory and a good grasp of the necessary techniques."

She dropped her eyes, murmuring, "Maybe. I'd never do it. I'm sorry I did it this time."

"Did you memorize everything, even the algorithms," Ana asked. She wondered if the young citizen would respond.

"I made some notes later, in my room."

"Why? Surely you wouldn't want to replicate it."

The young scientist looked miserable. "I wanted to understand it, to really understand it. I thought I might find an antidote if I could understand how it worked." She looked bleakly at Ana. "Do you understand?"

Ana understood. Just like her, Dorcas was a true scientist.

Changing the subject, Ana quizzed Dorcas about fusion power. She had an excellent theoretical and applied knowledge of the topic. In fact, Ana found her comments creative, even brilliant.

For the first time, Ana felt a spark of hope that she had found someone who could help her fight to dismantle the portal.

Despite their eagerness to return to the city, Ana, Colt, Piet, and Arlo were forced to remain in the dead city for a few days while the Conclave sent in functionaries to secure the facilities. They were questioned again and again about their knowledge of Chandler's plans. The Conclave were loath to believe that Chandler planned to destroy them but the evidence seemed pretty clear, especially when they found the protocols for creating the plague organisms in his penthouse office.

The Elders' representatives, in turn, were not entirely convinced by Colt's explanation for his presence in the dead city. His "hunch" that Ana was in the dead city contrasted, in their minds, with his taciturn, un-hunch-like demeanor. Colt, unmoved, worked out with Piet and the mercenary troops and Arlo explored the dead city, looking for his grandfather's residence.

Ana spent the time closeted with Dorcas, bringing the young scientist up to date about the portal.

Bartolo Bruxton was placed under house arrest, the functionaries less concerned about his alleged murder of Teegan than interested in what he knew about the Sojourner. He claimed he had not been aware that Councilor Besdine was the Sojourner, that he was not, himself, a religionist, but had brought Ana to the Councilor for the reward. He had, he maintained, killed Teegan when she attacked him in defense of Ana. Ana was hysterical; her word could not be relied upon.

Jordi, when he recovered from the fever brought on by drinking bad water, had to be restrained from running away into the dead city, vowing to find and kill all religionists. His health was still precarious and at Colt's suggestion he was airlifted, under guard, to the city and placed under Yonatan's care.

Consternation and chaos ruled the Citadel. Word of the events in the dead city quickly filtered throughout the body of elders and then into the consistory. As much as they would have liked, they knew they could not keep the story contained forever. But that was becoming a minor problem as they were confronted with a deeply concerning hailstorm of bad news. Citizens across the world were reporting small but unmistakable signs of disorder.

Several of the warlords in the hinterlands who were, by treaty, required to supply the Conclave with troops were moving armed militias away from their strongholds and closer to the planet's largest cities. Representatives of the Conclave were met with reassurances that the treaties would be honored. The militias, they almost universally claimed, were merely deployed on exercises to keep the soldiers sharp.

Inside the large cities, well-funded protest groups, espousing a range of vague goals and gripes, were coming together. Even more troubling, indications were that quantities of arms, including fusion weapons, were being clandestinely manufactured. The Conclave were more grateful than ever that they now had airships for reconnaissance. They could travel long distances and were largely silent and invisible at altitude. Moreover they could operate over water. What they saw was not encouraging. Several of the larger floating islands had been converted to bases for troops of uncertain origin. Moreover there were indications that the mysterious troops had both the necessary weapons for delivering moon busters and were operating airships of their own.

More and more citizens were talking about the ascension of the Sojourner.

40

In the city, Sparrow wiped the tears from his eyes using the sleeve from his kimono. Yonatan, looking as if he had aged ten years, stared somberly into a glass of something he presumed was alcoholic. He wasn't sure what it was, he had been drinking steadily since Sparrow placed it in front of him, without tasting and without any appreciable relief. He had sought out the House of Blue Leaves as a refuge from the demands of caring for Beau Lem and Jordi Petrie and from his own dark thoughts.

Sparrow had greeted him expansively and with his usual consideration and tact escorted him to a private table in the cafe.

Delicious small dishes and drinks appeared.

"Do you bring me news of our friends' adventures in the dead city? I've heard rumors that the Conclave was involved, that soldiers had been airlifted in."

Yonatan sighed. He had hoped Sparrow already knew about the deaths. He leaned forward, propping his head on his hand. "I can see you have not heard the bad news." He paused, hating the moment.

"Teegan Petrie and Linnet and Oren Mandible have all been killed."

"Linnet? Killed?" Sparrow shook his head in denial. He raised stricken eyes to Yonatan.

"I know very few details. I've been in constant contact with Piet regarding Beau's recovery and he told me. Also I have taken on the care of Jordi Petrie."

"Was he injured also?" Sparrow asked.

"He killed Linnet and her husband. He thought they were both religionists."

"Linnet had become a religionist?" Sparrow sounded doubtful.

"No. But apparently her husband was one."

"Surely that's no reason to kill someone. That sort of thing is left to the authorities and even then they usually just send them to re-education camps."

"Jordi's lost his mind, to use an old fashioned phrase. Teegan was apparently killed by a religionist, and he has decided to wage a personal war on all of them."

Sparrow looked up from his retsina. "I barely know the citizen. He and his wife were close to Colt and Ana, I think. I had heard that he was injured by Irene Thorne in the excitement in Deep Cove, but I thought he had recovered."

"In fact, Linnet nursed him back to health."

"Then why?"

"He hasn't a personality that can stand stress. Frankly I'm surprised he never became an addict of some kind. I understand he clung to Teegan even when she fooled around with other men, maybe she was his addiction. He believed she might have killed a digger, but he couldn't leave her. When he found himself in a highly dangerous situation in Deep Cove and was seriously injured, his mental health began to deteriorate. Then Ilsa, the wife of the owner of the villa, stirred him up with her fears about harboring Linnet's husband—they knew he was a religionist— and when Teegan was killed, he went to pieces. He killed Oren and Linnet then fled to the dead city where he expected to find Teegan's killer. Teegan's killer was apparently a healer at the local clinic. He decided this healer must be a religionist."

"And why would this healer kill Teegan? Was it jealousy?"

"I don't think so." Yonatan replied.

They sat in silence. Tears fell down Sparrow's fat cheeks.

"I had a great affection for Linnet," he dabbed at his eyes. "She had shown at lot of courage to run away to the city from the commune. The House of Blue Leaves was not a good fit for her but she made an effort. She was very young, you know. And she was fertile. She could have made a good living as a surrogate. But she was born under an unlucky star. First attracting the attention of Irene Thorne, then this."

"I don't know the details." Yonatan said. "Colt can fill us in when he returns to the city."

"If he returns to the city," Sparrow dabbed at his eyes. "He might be wise to stay away. The city is in turmoil. Conclave troops are everywhere; each new day brings stories of another atrocity. They have cleaned out the protestors' camp and carried the residents off to some hellhole of a re-education camp. Citizens who have resources are fleeing to the countryside, which I hear is now unsafe because of private militias that have strayed from their distant redoubts. There is talk of an uprising, but no one seems to know who is uprising and what their aim is."

"They are certainly challenging the Conclave," Yonatan said.

"Then they are doomed to fail. The Elders have the trained troops and weapons to destroy any usurper." Sparrow spoke with finality. "And they are ruthless."

"They are all of that." Yonatan thought with distaste about the suicide-inducing cockroaches he had passed on to Piet.

"I'm not sure they have not lost their respect for life," Yonatan said.

Sparrow looked shocked, then glanced around warily.

Suddenly he clapped his hands loudly, summoning a waiter.

Turning to Yonatan, he said, back in control of himself, "Let us have some food to anchor our spirits in the moment, leaving speculation about the motivations of the Elders to . . . ."

He turned and frowned as a waiter, an individual significantly older than those usually employed by Sparrow, approached. "Where's my personal waiter?" he snapped.

The waiter smiled at Sparrow then looked at Yonatan, favoring him with a glance that Yonatan thought was rather too appraising. The substitute waiter turned his attention back to Sparrow, reporting that the other waiter had gone to get a special item from the storeroom; he was, himself, merely helping out in the kitchen.

After Sparrow had given their orders and the waiter was returning to the kitchen, Yonatan made a questioning face after him.

"I'm convinced there are spies among the staff," Sparrow said. "Why and who they work for, I have no idea, but many of my compatriots report new staff suddenly appearing in their establishments replacing employees who suddenly have had to leave town or have taken sick with mysterious illnesses. It is very troubling."

"You've tried to investigate?"

"Oh, yes, but my remaining staff are frightened."

Yonatan sighed. "I'll be happy when Colt and Piet return to the city. Somehow I feel more secure when they are around."

"And Arlo," Sparrow said slyly.

Yonatan didn't reply.

41

In the dead city, the Conclave's functionaries were finally satisfied that the plague organisms were all destroyed and the facility thoroughly cleaned and ready to be returned to producing fuel. A small group of mercenaries remained to act as security for the facility and the remainder, with their commander, were ordered to return to the city. Piet caught a ride with them.

Arlo elected to remain in the dead city to continue searching for his grandfather's papers.

Colt and Ana expected to return to the city, accompanied by Dorcas. Ana was eager to get back to the Institute of Temporal Epistemology to check on the portal. Before they could depart, however, a functionary, newly arrived from the Citadel, sought her out and, obsequious and implacable, announced that she would accompany him back to meet with the Conclave. Immediately. Alone.

Even Colt could see that resistance was futile.

On his way back to the city to await Ana's return from the Conclave, Colt detoured to Deep Cove. He had promised Old Matley cash for picking him up under the pier, and he felt obligated to make the water rat whole for his efforts.

But first he stopped at Rick and Ilsa's villa. As he walked up to the door, he acknowledged a kind of depression that he had kept at bay during the days after the disappearance of Chandler and the destruction of the organisms. He felt dogged by the bitter sunlight; he felt a consuming free-floating fear, a need to go underground. He had a sense that his world and Ana's world was gone.

The villa had an odd feel. The door was locked, as usual, and no one answered his ring. He wandered around to the back of the villa where there was a slatted gate opening onto a stairs that led to the roof. This he easily vaulted and made his stealthy way up the stairs, listening for voices. He heard none. He ran lightly up the last of the stairs onto the back terrace, finding the doors to the interior also locked. The villa seemed deserted.

He made his way into the village of Deep Cove, seeking out the water rat who had helped him sneak into the dead city. Old Matley and his silent companion were at their customary place in the local tavern, drinking their foul green liquor, staring silently into space. Colt approached their table, waiting until Old Matley felt his presence, glanced up, startled.

"You still alive?" He pointed to a chair. No friendly fist bumping, Colt noted. Colt swung the chair around so he could see the entrance and sat.

"You wasn't there when we come to get you," Old Matley said.

"I was delayed."

"We heard there was some excitement, soldiers, helicopters in and out, some flying the Conclave flag."

The bartender brought over another carafe of the green swill for Old Matley and his companion and a vodka for Colt.

"You hear anything about my friends up at the villa?"

"They went back to the city where they come from."

"Why'd they do that? I thought they liked it here."

"Folks here didn't care for the goings on up at the villa. That citizen from the city murdered the housekeeper and her husband; they was religionists. Before that some other excitement with helicopters and citizens from the city making an uproar."

"I see." Colt said.

They drank. Colt let the silence gather.

"Anything else going on?" he asked.

The water rat looked up, considering his words.

"They say—and this is just a rumor—they say the Sojourner has risen."

The silent companion stirred, made an agitated squeak, and took a large drink.

"Oh?" Colt said. "What does that mean, do you think?"

The citizen pondered a while, weighing matters of trust and truth. Increasingly, under the New Dispensation, one did not say what one thought.

Finally he waved a hand at his companion, "she and I, we don't hold with religionism. It leads to trouble every time. And this Sojourner personage is big religionist trouble." Old Matley leaned toward Colt, dropping his voice, "He has troops on the floating islands, lots of them, and helicopters and air ships. We citizens who work the water see and hear but, mostly, we don't talk."

Colt did some leaning in himself. It took some self control. The water rat's breath was horrible. "What do you think he's planning?" Colt whispered.

Old Matley whispered back. "He's planning war. War on the Conclave."

He leaned back, looking resigned, speaking in a normal voice again.

"You want to know what I think. I think this Sojourner personage will bring on the end of the world. The plague started it and the Sojourner will finish it. I think it is the last days, the end of time."

Piet had been anxious to return to the city. He was in constant contact with Yonatan concerning Beau's condition, which remained largely unchanged. Piet felt he was the one who should be sitting at the bedside, that somehow his presence would lend his son strength. Also, when he was back with Grupo Uno he could channel their considerable planet-wide resources to finding and destroying the Sojourner, aka Chandler Besdine.

Between interrogations by the Conclave's functionaries, he and Colt had wiled away the time working out with the soldiers. While Colt and the soldiers had spent their evenings telling stories and playing a dice game that generated lots of laughter, Piet spent the evening hours at a spot he had found beyond the algae pools next to a real pond. The commander of the troops, who remained aloof from the dice games, occasionally accompanied him. They listened to the frogs and argued whether they were poisonous. The commander maintained that some citizens from her part of the world regarded them as a culinary delicacy; something Piet refused to believe. He found himself confiding in her his firm intention to find and destroy the Sojourner. He explained that he would never forget the cold evil flowing from the masked figure as he aimed his dagger, the wave of desire to wound, to cripple, to maximize pain for his son and, therefore, himself.

"Then," he said, "I realized I recognized the bastard. His mask blew aside and I saw the fighting ball. It was a citizen named Chandler Besdine, reportedly an intimate of the Elders."

"Why would the citizen injure your son rather than killing him outright? Have you done something to him?" she had asked reasonably.

"Not that I know of. I only met him last year briefly. He went to university with Colt and Ana."

"You're sure it was him?"

"I'm sure. He had Ana kidnapped and she saw him in the robe of the Sojourner."

"Maybe he enjoys causing pain," the commander mused. Then she had another thought. "But the Sojourner is a religionist. Many citizens follow him. Aren't religionists opposed to killing?"

"I can't believe Chandler is a religionist. If he is, he's a religionist who is willing to unleash the plague on the Elders and a lot of innocent citizens."

The commander shuddered.

"You think this Sojourner personage is planning an insurrection against the Conclave? So that religionism will be sanctioned?"

"I doubt that Chandler cares about religionism. If so, I expect only his religion will be sanctioned," Piet said.

The commander looked shocked. "But that's no different than the Conclave."

"No," Piet smiled unpleasantly. "And I know whose side I'm on."

"I don't like it." The commander said somberly.

"You're a soldier. You've been in battles."

She shook her head. "Not like this. Mostly we just fight against badly trained and armed religionist groups who run afoul of the Conclave or someone who ticks off our warlord. This is different." She paused, thinking. "This time we have to choose a side. The Conclave teaches that religionism leads to violence and despair." She paused again.

"I think they may be right."

42

The helicopter carrying Ana to the Citadel sped across the countryside, casting a shadow on the empty fields below. She found the experience of flying exhilarating; their contacts with the Conclave had always been carried out by Elvistine, and he usually traveled by aircar. She wondered how it would feel to float in one of the great air ships. Quieter, at least. The helicopter was very noisy. She had tried to question the functionary who was accompanying her, but he was worried and taciturn. Ignoring her, he frowned through the window at the vast empty spaces below.

She wondered whom she was meeting. When she pressed the functionary, he merely shook his head and continued glaring at the landscape. It mattered little, of course, because the identity and number of elders were kept from the citizenry. She once more wondered whether Chandler was an elder or, as he claimed, merely a member of the consistory, the vast bureaucratic apparatus that supported the Conclave and ran the world. Since he had apparently been trusted to travel freely, she was inclined to believe he was actually an Elder. She also wondered if anyone among the Elders knew about his Sojourner persona.

The Citadel, when they finally arrived, was situated on a mountaintop, a cluster of white domes and minarets. Spread down the sides of the mountain and onto the plains below was a vast city. Chandler's deadly plague would have destroyed not only the elders but also most of the city's residents. How far it would have spread beyond the city, carried by panicked citizens fleeing to imagined havens of safety, was anyone's guess. It was highly contagious.

Without the Conclave and the consistory, the world would have quickly succumbed to starvation and the violent internecine warfare that was so prominent among the old people.

The helicopter settled gracefully on a high terrace at the very top of the Citadel. Once the rotors were stilled, the door was opened by a young citizen who grinned cheerfully and took her backpack and brief case. He was so young she wondered whether he could possibly be an Elder, but when the functionary who had accompanied her on the flight first fist bumped then touched his forehead in a gesture of respect, she decided she must indeed be in the presence of a member of the Conclave of Elders.

The young citizen chirped at her, making small talk, asking about her trip, was she hungry, would she like to lie down. He escorted her into the cool dark interior of the Citadel. He led her through a series of passages, tiled in subtly-colored stones with walls of beautiful hardwoods inset with silver motifs. "Beautiful, isn't it," he said over his shoulder. "In the old days, it was the residence of a king."

Eventually they reached a small, elegant guest suite and the elder suggested she relax for a few minutes. He pointed out the bar and small cooler. If she wanted food, he started to say, but she shook her head.

"I'm too excited to eat," she said.

He grinned. "It won't be long. They're setting up a meeting room now."

When he had gone, Ana looked longingly at the sonic shower, she felt gritty and dusty after her ride in the helicopter. Before she could act a light tap at the door signaled the presence of yet another elder, this one tall and slender with striking blue eyes that seemed incongruous with his long dark robe and soft boots like those usually worn by dark-eyed desert dwellers.

"Dr. Bede," he spoke with a slight indefinable accent, "please join the Conclave of Elders at your convenience."

"I think now would be perfectly convenient," Ana said, following him through the door.

As she trailed behind the elder through a long sequence of cool, dimly lit corridors, the only sound the swishing skirts of the elder's long robe, Ana began to feel a sense of calm repose. Their pace seemed to slow, to become more meditative, less urgent. One felt, she thought, as though this were the center of the world where all problems were solved. The floor was gently rising and she was not surprised when they emerged onto another high terrace. At this point, evening had begun to fall and the sky had assumed a hazy luminance. The circular area was ringed by white columns and lighted with a scattering of small hidden lamps. Six chairs were arranged in a circle, with four occupied by personages who rose when she entered, waiting courteously for her to be seated.

Looking around at the group, Ana was irresistibly reminded of numerous meetings she had attended over the years. With the exception of her blue-eyed guide, those present were older and displayed the gravitas, the unconscious self-importance of tenured professors. At least one had the look of a grandmotherly crèche worker. All wore conventional clothing; disappointingly none wore the white robes depicted in her childhood books.

After she and her blue-eyed guide were seated, one of the personages, a little, bald, desiccated individual spoke in a dusty voice, "Dr. Bede, I speak for all elders present, when I thank you for joining us here at the Citadel. It's an honor for us to meet with someone of your brilliance, and we want to personally thank you for your work in destroying the plague organisms. We are more indebted to you, your husband, and your companions than we can express." The personage, who Ana assumed was chairing the meeting, continued in this vein for a few more paragraphs and Ana began to realize there was a coda, a big "but" coming at the end.

While he droned on, she looked curiously at the others. In books, they were portrayed in white robes, bald, sexless, and sometimes with a third eye indicating, the citizenry were told, that they possessed special powers. So far only the white Citadel resembled anything in the early books. No one wore white robes, and only the chairman was bald and that was surely a function of his great age. Two were female personages and none revealed a third eye. So,

Ana thought sadly, no special powers.

"Now that the threat of the plague has been removed, we need to move on to a more important matter," the chairman continued.

"I still think the war is more important," someone grumbled.

Ana's blue-eyed guide spoke up, "you know we agreed that we can easily defeat the so-called Sojourner and his troops."

"Anyone who follows a leader wearing a mask is a fool," one of the elders, a stocky chap built like a wrestler, said sententiously.

"Yes, but Chandler Besdine is no fool," another said.

"Obviously," the chairman snapped, "but that is not why we asked Dr. Bede here today. She is not an expert in warfare. We rely on you for that." He nodded to the sententious one.

"Well then?" another elder barked. "Get on with it."

The chairman nodded to Ana, "Perhaps you can share your concerns about the portal," he said.

Ana then related the same account of the portal that she had shared with Chandler. The elders, looking grim, also reflected various shades of disbelief.

"If this is true, how can you be so calm?" one asked.

"Because if you think of it too deeply, it can drive you over the edge of sanity into despair. As it did Desmond Elvistine." Ana thought sadly, as it would me, if I thought there was no hope. "Also," she added, dryly, "I've been distracted."

An elder who had seemed half asleep suddenly

stirred, "Ah, Elvistine. What exactly did happen to Elvistine? We were planning a full scale investigation into his disappearance, but we have also been distracted." He glared at Ana then looked grimly around the group, as if blaming them for the distraction.

Another elder, who had also not so far contributed to the conversation, smiled at Ana and spoke softly with a charming accent, "We had heard that, in your presence, he opened another portal and disappeared through it."

"I suppose Chandler told you that?" Ana said.

The elder did not respond. Her eyes were not so charming, she looked sharply at Ana. "Never mind who told us. Did that really happen? You were with him at the clinic."

"He was badly injured in the aircar accident," Ana temporized. She had hoped to avoid this discussion.

They all looked at her and said nothing.

Ana sighed, "I made a promise to Desmond that I would not tell what happened. He didn't want anyone to know. He was ashamed."

"Ashamed of what?" the chairman waved a hand impatiently.

"He suicided. He had a fusion pistol and he suicided. He begged me not to tell people that he had destroyed himself. His was a firm belief held over from the old days that self-murder is wrong."

"That's ridiculous," someone snapped. "A scientist of Elvistine's brilliance. . . ."

Ana continued, "He wasn't thinking clearly. He had a heart condition and his injuries pushed him over the edge. He had been distraught for some time.

"Perhaps you can explain a little about Elvistine's

state of mind," the chairman prodded her.

"As you no doubt know, Desmond and Menard Tillman together developed the technology that would make fusion energy accessible. With the refinement of the techniques, he became enchanted with the uses for this seemingly inexhaustible power. He had been interested in the concept of parallel realities for years and when I went to work for him at the Institute of Temporal Epistemology, our calculations seemed to confirm the existence of multiple realities, each on a slightly different time line. Desmond was convinced that with fusion energy we could access at least one of them.

"We refined our calculations at the institute, but when we opened the initial small portal, all that happened was the emission of some kind of radiant energy. We were busy with other projects at that time, projects for the Conclave." Ana paused and looked meaningfully at the assembled elders.

"Elvistine seemed to lose interest. He said it was just a scientific oddity, interesting but useless."

"Of course," Ana grimaced, "we couldn't close it."

She continued. "We were annoyed when one of the assistants leaked the story to the video outlets and riled up the anti-ephemerists. So Desmond leaked his own story that the institute was working on a project to destroy time. He thought citizens would conclude he was delusional and forget the portal.

Ana sighed, "I thought he had lost interest permanently. That we could return to our ongoing projects. But then he visited the Conclave and came back re-inspired." It was Ana's turn to give the elders the stink eye.

"He came back with the idea that we needed to

project more energy through the portal. He made some tweaks to the generator," Ana paused here, looking annoyed, "he wouldn't share his calculations."

"Then, through the auspices of the Conclave, we suddenly had access to tremendous quantities of fusion power. We poured more and more power into the portal and it did grow. But it still did not reveal parallel dimensions."

"And the control of time?" the chairman was on the edge of his seat.

"Inside the portal, time does not exist." Ana said simply.

This confounded them all.

"Are you sure," an elder said carefully, "that this is not just a very strong black hole in which time is so slow as to be imperceptible?"

"I am not sure," Ana said. "But the point is moot. Whatever you want to term the portal, a black hole, an extreme entropy sink, it is growing and at its margins the bonds that hold our world together are disappearing. Whatever it touches disappears."

They sat in silence. Finally the soldier said softly to the chairman, "is this true, chairman?"

The chairman hesitated, then shrugged, "It appears so."

"How fast is it growing?" another asked.

"Slowly, but the rate of growth seems to be increasing."

"It isn't exponential, is it?" the grandmotherly elder asked.

"Don't be stupid. If it were, we'd all be gone in short order," one of the elders snapped at her.

Ana didn't think it was a stupid question but she said nothing; they were not scientists. She was surprised that only the chairman had seemed aware of the issue. She realized she herself had been swayed by the Conclave's claims of omniscience.

"The question, of course, is what we are going to do about it. Can it be stopped?" the soldier said.

The chairman smiled at Ana, "That is the question. And that is why we asked Dr. Bede to join us today. She can answer that question. Well, Dr. Bede, can we save the world?"

"Maybe," Ana said. "I've been working on it when I have time. I need to get back to the institute, I need computing capacity, and I need help."

The Elders all looked at each other appraisingly. Ana waited. Finally the chairman said, "Tell me, Dr. Bede, how many of the calculations were developed by Dr. Elvistine alone?"

"You mean without my assistance," Ana snapped. "I'm very capable of carrying on his work."

"I'm not questioning your abilities. I'm asking if Elvistine had assistance from anyone else. Did the ideas originate with him?"

Ana thought about it for a few seconds.

"As I said earlier, in the beginning he developed some of the basic work while he was collaborating with Dr. Menard Tillman on the moon-buster."

The chairman looked around him at the other elders, conveying an unspoken question. Ana noted that each one nodded silently.

"Have you given any thought to the team you would want to work on this project," the chairman said, changing the subject, Ana thought. The chairman continued without irony, "This saving-the-world-project."

Ana named a couple of deep scientists who

worked at Conclave laboratories and included Dr. Dorcas Wovoka, who had impressed her so deeply with her work on the plague culture.

The chairman, nodded. "I'm not familiar with Dr. Wovoka, but, if she graduated from one of our training facilities, she must be competent, and I trust your judgment. The other two you name are not exactly up to your level or that of Dr. Elvistine, were he still alive."

"No. Few people are our level," Ana said.

"What about Menard Tillman?" the chairman asked.

"Dr. Tillman?" Ana was shocked. "Desmond considered him the most brilliant scientist of all. I never worked with him. At university I worked only with Dr. Elvistine. He considered Tillman even more brilliant than himself. But, what difference does it make? He's dead." Suddenly she became excited. "Do you have his notes, his papers. They could be very helpful."

"In fact, we have the personage himself," the chairman said with satisfaction.

"He is completely insane, dangerous," the soldier growled. "He's under twenty four hour guard."

"But his intelligence is unimpaired," the chairman said.

Ana was stunned. Tillman alive but insane. She felt hope, faintly but unmistakably. She and Dorcas and Tillman might be able to close the portal.

They all silently watched while Ana assessed the implications.

Finally, one of the elders said, "Dr. Bede didn't finish the story," interrupting her thoughts. She looked up, startled.

"Why did Dr. Elvistine commit suicide? What was he ashamed of?"

"I don't know if I can explain it," Ana finally said.

"Try." This from the elder with the velvety voice and the ice-cold eyes.

Ana gathered her thoughts. "Desmond Elvistine was a genius and like all geniuses, he was wildly imaginative. He could visualize abstractions like no one else," here Ana paused and looked at the surrounding elders, "like almost no one else and render them into mathematical constructs that would enable less gifted citizens to reify them.

"He was also eccentric. For example, he believed he was more creative when his mind was exhausted, that rigorous thought could lead the mind away from the intuitive insights necessary for breakthroughs. When he expanded the portal the second time, he was baffled. He could not wrap his mind around the idea of nothingness, of absence. He pushed himself to mental and physical exhaustion, time and time again. Then when it became clear that the portal was growing inexorably, he began to feel guilt because he had become the destroyer of the world. As we fruitlessly sought a way to close the portal, he despaired. Then Chandler's comments to my husband convinced him that Dr. Tillman was working on a parallel path and was trying to open a portal himself. He had thought Tillman was either dead or in stasis, and he had no doubt that Dr. Tillman was capable. Our calculations indicated that a second portal would cause reality to be completely annihilated in a matter of minutes. He dashed off to the Citadel to warn them, to warn you, but he was attacked before he could arrive.

"He must have communicated with someone at the Citadel before he was attacked because when I saw him in the clinic he was in deepest despair. He seemed to think that Dr. Tillman was on the brink of opening a second portal and if that occurred the dissolution of the world would be his fault.

"He was irrational. Crying. I didn't know what to do. He told me he was going to destroy himself and begged me not to tell anyone, to make up a story. Before I could act, he took out his fusion pistol and destroyed himself. I had noticed a supply closet across the hallway so I grabbed some cleaning supplies and started a fire, threw a full can of chemicals on the fire starting a small explosion. I hoped it would satisfy the hospital staff. Then I hurried to Deep Cove to tell Colt what had happened. When I saw many other people present, I blurted out the first thing that came to mind, that Prof. Elvistine had opened a portal."

"And that it meant Armageddon," one of the elders observed.

"It does mean Armageddon, if we can't find a way to close the portal," Ana said.

"I guess this illustrates one thing, then," the chairman looked around at the assembled elders, "the anti-ephemerists are right. Deep science will destroy the world."

43

For Piet, getting back to the Subs was a return to reality. He felt himself again.

When the soldiers' transport helicopter had landed, the commander had said, "Mind if I come with you? They told me to keep an eye on you."

"They?" he had answered and she had rolled her eyes. "Who else," she said. Which did not, of course, answer his question. Still he didn't mind her company. Having access to her troops might be a boon and, in the Subs, he would be in control, he could lose her any time.

His first stop, even before checking up on his trailer, was to see Beau. A haggard Yonatan had good news. They had deemed Beau strong enough to remove him from the chemical coma, and he was conscious. Still weak, he grinned at his dad, and raised a thin arm in greeting. Piet sat beside him, a hand on his son's shoulder, trying to stifle long-held tears.

Behind them, Piet heard the commander introduce

herself to Yonatan and ask after Jordi, whom some of her soldiers had escorted to the clinic. In the background, Yonatan told her that Jordi was physically recovered but still mentally unsound. They were planning to send him to a rest home in the countryside for treatment.

Beau wanted to hear everything that had happened. He knew nothing of Piet's trip to the dead city or of Chandler Besdine assuming the role of Sojourner. But he tired easily, and seemed subdued. Troubled by his apparent lassitude, Piet filled him in on some of the details and promised to return soon.

Before he could stand up, Beau put a hand on his arm and grinned feebly, rolling his eyes. "Is that your new girlfriend? She's beautiful." He looked toward the commander.

Piet laughed. "No, she's too young for me. Maybe when you're up and around, you can get to know her."

At that moment, Piet thought he saw Beau give Yonatan a troubled glance.

He looked back at his father and said, sadly, "I'm pretty sure she wouldn't be interested in me."

As they left, Piet asked Yonatan about Beau.

"It's only a matter of time," Yonatan said. "He's a young citizen, he'll bounce back."

"He seems depressed," Piet said.

Yonatan looked away, "It's just a side effect of the injury. He'll be okay."

They agreed to meet at the House of Blue Leaves later.

As they walked toward Piet's home in the Subs, Piet said to the commander, "What did you think of Yonatan?"

She looked puzzled at his question. "Why? Don't you trust him?"

"It's not exactly that. I can't explain." He responded.

She shrugged. "I think he's got a lot on his mind. He seemed very troubled, very concerned."

Piet thought about the suicide cockroaches that he had received from Yonatan, remembered Yonatan's revulsion at the idea of being the agent of such despair.

"Yeah," he said. "Do you think he and Beau are— you know—lovers?"

The commander looked amused. "You don't like the idea?"

"I guess it's because Yonatan is so much older than Beau. Beau hasn't had a chance to live yet, to have experiences."

She laughed and patted his arm. "Spoken like parents have from the beginning of time."

"Were you raised by your parents?" Piet changed the subject.

"No. We were raised in crèches, but our parents were around all the time. My father was a teacher in the school."

He stopped walking and looked at her. "You know, Beau is right. You are kind of beautiful."

She laughed again.

She was too young for him.

Sparrow was consumed with curiosity about the events in the dead city. Rumors had flown around the city, among all levels of society, wild rumors about the massing of warlords, airships, and thousands following a mysterious personage known as the

Sojourner. Sparrow had gone so far as to personally leave the House of Blue Leaves to mingle with some of his compatriots who catered to the elite classes. He also dispatched some of his young workers to mingle with truck drivers and other rough elements to hear their rumors, which often provided more information than those from citizens isolated in the top strata of society.

He was delighted therefore to see Piet and a female citizen in an unfamiliar but, unmistakably military, uniform, enter his establishment.

Piet introduced his companion, laughing, "she's spying on me for the Conclave."

Sparrow hustled them to his private table in the cafe. At his gesture, waiters brought glasses for his favorite special retsina and numerous delicacies.

The commander, impressed, complimented his hospitality.

"We've finally begun to get deliveries from the countryside," he waved a fat hand covered with rings. Piet had warned her about Sparrow's largely unsanctioned mode of dress and she found herself fascinated by his get up. "Who knows what will happen when the war starts."

"You're convinced there will be a war?" Piet asked.

"Aren't you? Did you learn something in the dead city that convinces you otherwise?" Sparrow asked.

"You don't think the Conclave will easily put down the Sojourner's forces, like any other religionist uprising?"

"I don't know, friend Piet. I have heard there are factions within the Conclave who may be using this as an opportunity to gain power. No one is sure just who in the Conclave the various warlords are following. The Conclave may no longer speak with one voice."

"Maybe the Conclave should be overthrown."

Everyone looked to the speaker in shock. Yonatan had approached the table unnoticed, even by the commander, who continued to be mesmerized by Sparrow's rings and the beaded fringe on his sleeves.

"Healer Belasco," Sparrow heaved himself to his feet. "You are fortunate you are among friends." He pulled out a chair for Yonatan.

"But I am among friends," Yonatan said. He looked around the table, his gaze lingering on the commander.

"Now Piet can bring us up to date on his adventures in the dead city. Before he begins, a question. When can we expect to see friend Colt Bede back in the city?" Sparrow poured Yonatan a glass of wine and pushed forward a dish of Yonatan's favorite stuffed figs.

"Colt is staying in the dead city until Ana returns from the Conclave. I don't know why she was summoned, but she was. Maybe they wanted to thank her in person." Piet said.

"For what?" Sparrow asked.

"Now that's a long story," Piet took a healthy swig of retsina, wishing it were cognac, and began.

44

Colt, himself, was not quite sure why he remained in the dead city. He had planned to visit Deep Cove to pay off Old Matley then catch a ride back to the city to await Ana's return. The departure of Rick and Ilsa to the city had not changed his mind nor had Old Matley's stories about the massing of the Sojourner's forces. Still he found himself returning to the dead city from Deep Cove, having once again taken advantage of Old Matley's skiff.

He commandeered Chandler's penthouse suite and continued whiling away the time training with the small group of bored mercenaries who had been left behind to secure the refinery. All the scientists had moved on, and the lab building felt abandoned and dusty. He usually had dinner at the pension with Arlo, who was still combing through his grandfather's papers looking for, Colt guessed, some kind of enlightenment.

Then one evening Arlo did not arrive and, when he didn't call or communicate, Colt went to Arlo's grandfather's house. It was empty. Then Colt realized why he had stayed in the dead city—it was to keep an eye on Arlo and he had failed. Arlo was gone, no one knew where.

Colt went for a walk beyond the algae beds to an open marshy space away from his fellow citizens. He missed Ana but for once wasn't worried about her. As long as the C.E. needed her, she should be safe. He hated the idea that Rick and Ilsa had to flee back to the city from their safe haven in the countryside because they were viewed by the citizens of Deep Cove as possibly inviting attention from the authorities. That was a flaw in the perfection of the New Dispensation. He missed Teegan, senselessly murdered, and Jordi, damaged, not hopefully beyond repair. And Linnet . . . he had loved Linnet, brave, compassionate Linnet, another victim of fear. Meanwhile Chandler Besdine still lived, planning to wreak some kind of vengeful firestorm upon multitudes of innocent people. This time, for Colt, it would be, if necessary, a fight to the death.

As he walked further away from the dead city, the sky brightened. Maybe he was coming to actually like the countryside.

Suddenly he noticed, walking cautiously toward him, two giant birds. The only wild animals Colt had ever seen close up were a few feral cats who had escaped the authorities' ban. These birds were tall, almost to his chest, with long, sharp beaks and small eyes. They walked with an odd thrusting gait, lifting their long legs high in the air. As they drew closer, they noticed Colt. The lead bird stopped and, cocking its head slightly cast an appraising look, locking eyes.

Colt felt a thrill as wordless, elemental intelligence passed between them. Satisfied of his benign intentions, they continued on their way. Slowly, dignified and purposeful.

Enthralled, Colt watched them out of sight. They were the most glorious things he had ever seen in his life.

ABOUT THE AUTHOR

A career bureaucrat, Rachel Winters retired to Central Florida where she lives with her husband and two Chihuahuas. When not writing deeply existential science fiction, she plays Mah Jongg and plans trips to remote spots around the world.